Try Not to Die

With Satan Inside

Mark Tullius

VINCERE
P R E S S

Published by Vincere Press
65 Pine Ave., Ste 806
Long Beach, CA 90802

Try Not to Die: With Satan Inside

Printed in the United States of America
First Edition

ISBN: 9781961740501
Cover by Jun Ares

A Warning from the Author

While *Try Not to Die: With Satan Inside* isn't as graphic or intense as *Try Not to Die: In This Damned House*, it still earns its place as the second Extreme Horror Edition. The last thing I want as an author and publisher is to blindside readers who aren't ready for disturbing material, so consider this your fair warning.

This story contains sex, violence, strong language, and religious themes. My goal was never to attack the Catholic Church or any faith, but to keep the story grounded in something that feels real. As I learned while writing this, Satan is kind of a dick, and a cruel one at that. Take what he does with a grain of salt, but don't rub it in your wounds. That'd only make him happy.

You'll also notice there's no survivor version of this book. Early on, the story splits into three distinct paths, and in some cases, survival just isn't on the table. This would've made for the shortest survivor version yet, and honestly, I want you to face those uncomfortable choices head-on.

Because this is a shorter entry in the series, I'm continuing Satan's misadventures through an extreme horror anthology featuring other *Try Not to Die* authors—Wrath James White, Duncan Ralston, Candace Nola, Robert Essig, Andrew Najberg, Kevin David Anderson, Megan Stockton, Steve Stred, Brennan LaFaro, and Timothy King. Andrew's story is included as a bonus at the end of this book.

Now go forth and let a little darkness in. Amen.

Mark

Micha,

Your twisted imagination and sharp insights pushed this book to darker, stranger places than I could have reached alone. Thank you for helping me fly through the pages and for making every death scene that much more disturbingly delicious.

Try Not to Die
With Satan Inside

The sun slowly sinks below the horizon, the last bits of light flickering off the rolling waves. With the clear skies and cool temperature, I couldn't have asked for a better setting, Farina's small patio all to ourselves. Beth and I have been enjoying watching people stroll by on the sidewalk, the street quiet except occasional passing cars. Both our meals were excellent, and the two bottles of red wine are giving me the confidence to follow through with my plan.

Leanne, our waitress, whose every curve is displayed in her black mini-skirt and matching top, brings us a large slice of tiramisu with two spoons. "Is there anything else I can get for you?" She leans in, brushing my shoulder as she removes the empty wine bottle from the table. "Another one?" she asks, only looking at me, her million-dollar smile not hiding the hurt I caused over a year ago.

"No thanks. Just the check would be great."

"You got it," she says, walking back into the restaurant.

If I had known Leanne was working here, I never would have gotten reservations, for her sake as well as mine. But none of that matters. All that matters is what's in my pocket and how Beth reacts.

Beth runs a hand through her blonde bob cut. "You fucked her," she says like a fact, her narrowed eyes never leaving mine.

I gulp hard, because it is a fact and denying it would make me a liar. I just wasn't expecting Beth to bring it up even though she's been watching Leanne's every move since we got here. Probably because of my dumb ass stumbling and bumbling when Leanne greeted us at the entrance. The whole 'Oh shit, Lee, when did you start working here,' might have given something away.

"Well?" Beth asks, eyebrows raised.

"It was nothing. A long time ago."

"I bet," she says, not buying it.

Keeping it short, I explain how I'd broken it off with Leanne as soon as I realized she wanted me more than I wanted her. My M.O. of hurting people early so I wouldn't wreck them later.

Beth doesn't look convinced. "Really?"

"She didn't have what I needed. What I wanted." I take hold of Beth's hands and gaze deep into her beautiful blue eyes. "She wasn't you. I want you."

Beth chuckles. "Have I ever told you how cute you are when you're embarrassed?"

I blow out a breath and use my napkin to dab my forehead dry. "Once or twice," I say, thrilled she's just messing with me. "So, you're not mad?"

"What right would I have being mad about someone you were with before me? Even if she is freaking hot as hell."

"Some people trip on those things. And she's got nothing on you. You're beautiful."

"And hot?" she asks with a sly smile.

"Goddamn, you have no idea. Every time we leave the apartment, I'm prepared to beat the shit out of every dude I catch drooling over your ass."

"Aw, how sweet."

I try the tiramisu, mushing it around in my mouth because it's Beth's favorite, but anything coffee-flavored grosses me out.

"Well, you don't have to worry about me," she says, scooping up another bite. "I'm secure enough to not worry even though I'm sure she'd welcome you back with open legs."

I laugh, my mouthful of mush spraying the table. "We need to go drinking more often," I say, surprised by this side of her, the stress of her job often keeping her a bit anxious and uptight.

"I bet you say that to all the girls." She goes in for another bite, licks her lips.

I wipe up my mess and set my spoon down. "Nope, you're the only one for me," I say, summoning the nerve to finally ask her what I really want to. Is it the smartest move? So many of our friends swear they'll never marry, that there's no point. My parents' marriages were shitty too, five of their six resulting in divorces, the last in death.

"You okay?" she asks. "You're sweating again."

My heart is racing and my palms are clammy, but I do my best to play it off. "Just one of the drawbacks of having a shaved head. No hair to sop up the sweat."

Beth takes another bite of tiramisu while I wage an internal battle, worried she'll say no and our relationship will be ruined. And just as worried she'll say yes and we'll both live to regret it.

I wipe my hands on my jeans, reach into my left pocket, and wrap my hand around the small box. "Do you remember our first date here?"

"Of course. I'll never forget that night."

"You remember telling me your childhood dream of getting married down the street at St. Mark's?"

She shakes her head. "No. How embarrassing."

"Well," I say, taking the box out of my pocket. I get up from my chair and kneel beside her. "I'd be honored if you let me make that dream come true."

Beth gasps, her eyes wide, tears welling up.

I open the box to show her the diamond ring that practically cost me three months of pay. "Will you marry me?"

"Oh my God. Yes, yes, yes." She pushes her chair back so she can hug me and nearly bowls me over.

We stand and I kiss her so hard I hope she feels every bit of my love, my desire to spend the rest of my life with her.

I break off the kiss and give her one last squeeze. "I promise I'll spend my life making you happy," I say, slipping the ring on her finger.

She stares at me with the sweetest smile. "And so do I."

I walk back to my chair and have a seat, loving how genuinely happy she looks, all the tension and worry of work magically gone. A huge cockroach scurries past my foot and under the table. Before it reaches Beth's side and scares her, I crush it, the crunch grossing me out.

Leanne enters the patio to drop off the bill and mints. "What's going on here?" she asks, taking in the scene. "Oh my gosh, did you guys just get engaged?"

Both of us nod, the words not coming.

"Well, let me take a photo for you." She holds out her hand for my phone.

I give it to her and scoot my chair over so I'm side by side with Beth who rests her head on my shoulder.

Leanne snaps a few photos and hands me back my phone. "Congratulations. You make such a beautiful couple. Really."

"Thanks, Lee," I say, feeling like maybe this was the closure she needed.

Leanne heads back inside while Beth selects the best photo and forwards it to herself. "I'll post it later, if that's okay."

"Absolutely. I want to shout this to the world. You just made me the luckiest man alive."

Beth kisses my cheek and admires the ring while I take care of the bill. I leave a big tip to thank Leanne for being so great, opting for cash so we don't have to stick around.

"So what should we do?" I ask. "We can go down the street to The Rusty Knife to celebrate with a few drinks or grab a ride and head home."

"I'm good with either."

Beth makes decisions all day at work as a charge-nurse, so she likes it when I choose for us. With Billy bartending tonight, we'd have a blast at The Knife, but we both already have a little buzz and can just go home and fuck.

Grab a drink at the bar. Turn to page 72.

Go home and fuck. Turn to page 12.

This is too much. I'm about to kill the only person I've ever truly loved. I've hurt her more tonight than I've hurt anyone in my life. "Stop," I say. "She's better."

The priests don't listen. They just keep shouting prayers and demanding that Satan leave her body.

"He's already gone." I turn to Father Paul. "You have to stop!"

He shakes his head. "Satan is still inside her."

Tears pour as she looks at me, sucking at the air. "Can't breathe."

With the blanket wrapped around her arms and Luke holding her ankles, there's no harm in me getting my weight off her. I roll to the side and put my back to the wall beside Father James, ready to grab her if I need to.

"Restrain her," Father Paul orders James. "And do not release her legs!" he tells Luke, who is down on his knees, Beth's ankles held tight under each armpit.

Beth has already wriggled a good way out of the homeless guy's sheet. She pulls her body down and raises her arms up, shucking the restraint. James grabs her wrist, but that doesn't do anything but piss Beth off. She does the quickest crunch and punches Luke in the face, shattering his glasses and breaking his nose.

I fucked up big time and need to fix this. I try to grab hold of Beth, but she's already standing on the bed, both hands free. I dive for her legs, but she jumps and grabs hold of the ceiling fan. I look up from the bed, see the fan hold for a second before it breaks from the ceiling, all of Beth's weight landing on my lower back. Chunks of plaster clatter down around us along with the fan mount and a snapped blade.

Father Luke crawls out of the bedroom while Father Paul keeps shouting his prayer, and James uses the bottle and his hand for a makeshift cross like he's trying to hold back a vampire. Keeping me pinned on the bed, Beth scoops up a broken fan blade. She swings away, the jagged edge slicing open James's pajama shirt and his belly, releasing a river of blood.

The priest crumples to the floor and Beth jumps off me, landing beside him. I get up on all fours and lunge for her, but she slips the tackle and I smash into the wall.

Paul waves the crucifix back and forth in front of Beth, who's standing there with a smile. "Stay back, demon!"

"Your little cross is as powerful as your prayers," Satan says, a hellish voice that makes me stay down. "Bow down to me and I'll let you live," he tells Paul.

Father Paul's face turns red and he raises the crucifix like a hammer. "I'll kill you!" he shouts, swinging for her head.

Beth sidesteps the blow and jumps on him, burying her face in his neck. Father Paul screams, but not for long. Beth whips her head back and forth, breaking off with a giant piece of flesh between her teeth, blood spraying all over her face.

The crucifix clatters to the floor. Father Paul falls beside it, blood pouring out from the gaping hole in his throat.

I back into the corner, put my hands up in front of me. "Please," I say through tears. "Just leave us. Leave Beth."

Beth spits the meat onto the bed. "Just the two of us. The perfect end to such a romantic night."

The only way to end this is to kill her, the only weapon a few feet away. I scramble for the crucifix. Beth gets there first, her shin connecting with my jaw, the break so loud. So painful.

She wraps the bed sheet around her hand and picks up the crucifix, steam rising from it.

I can't speak with my shattered jaw, but it wouldn't matter anyway. I try to cover my skull because I see where she's aiming. But again, nothing matters.

The correct choice was to finish the exorcism.

Turn to page 43.

The absolute last thing I want to do right now is go check on some dude in the bathroom. If I don't go, however, there's a good chance Beth will do it on her own, especially since she's been drinking. So, I say, "Sure thing," not bothering to tell her the real reason I'm going is because I've got to piss anyhow. "Be right back."

She rises up on her stool to give me a little kiss. "Thank you."

When I step away from the bar, the shots hit. I'm drunker than I'd like. Careful not to bump into anyone, I make it to the hallway where I keep my hand on the wall to help with balance.

Glass-framed photos of the Lancers' championship football teams line both sides of the hallway. We were the champs my senior year, which was a decade ago, but I never look at the photo. It's just a painful reminder of my potential and how quickly it was stripped from me with a blown knee. There's no guarantee I would've gone on to college or the pros, but goddamn I would have loved a shot to be someone special.

Near the end of the hall, just outside the women's restroom, two ladies are admiring each other's tattoos. "Oh my God, how gorgeous. I love flowers," the skinny one in leopard print says, slurring her words. "So real, I can almost smell it."

The bigger gal in black praises her tattoo artist, saying how long she had to wait to be seen by him. Too bad the piece looks like it could have been done in prison. And I'm pretty sure that flowery scent is her nasty perfume mixed with body odor.

But I'm not a dick and keep these thoughts to myself, waiting one more second to see if they'll notice me and realize they're blocking the way. They don't, so I say, "Excuse me, ladies. Can I sneak by?"

The skinny one's irritated, but flower girl flashes a crooked smile as she checks me out from head to toe. "Oh, yummy," she says, leaving just enough room so I'll brush up against them.

I nod and squeeze past. The restroom's fairly small, but it's still clean thanks to it being so early. The urinals are the kind that go all the way to the floor, and no one is at them. Two of the three stalls are closed, however.

Now that I'm in here, I really have to piss. I head over to the first urinal and let loose a stream, listening to an argument in the middle stall. I assume he's on speakerphone until I realize it's the same person talking; he's just holding one side of the conversation in a much deeper voice.

"No, no, no," the guy snivels as if about to cry.

I zip up and wash my hands, using the mirror to confirm it's the bloody shoe guy in there, the other closed stall empty.

"You'll do whatever I fucking tell you," he says in the slower, scary voice.

The guy grunts and lets out a small cry. "No. Don't do this," he begs.

"You have no say."

I wad up my paper towel and chuck it in the trash. "Hey, bud." I walk up to the stall. "You doing okay?"

"Just leave me," the guy cries.

I don't know if he's talking to me or himself. He hadn't looked drunk, but he must be high on something. Or maybe he's having some kind of schizophrenic breakdown or a stroke like Beth said.

I knock on the stall. "Just got to check on you. Cover up if you don't want me to see anything." As I reach over the door to unlatch it, there's a sharp cry of pain.

"Help me!" he says, sounding so scared.

I swing open the door, stunned by what's in front of me. The glasses guy is on the toilet, steak knife in one hand, three lines of flayed skin torn through his forearm, the blood soaking his slacks.

He looks up at me with furious eyes, a flash of red around his pupils. A sick smile. "Sorry, this soul's occupied."

I can't let this nutjob kill himself, and no way I'm turning my back on a crazy fucker with a weapon. I reach down for his knife hand, but he's fast and whips the blade around, slicing into my palm.

"Fuck!" I back up and lose my balance, landing hard on my ass. My good hand holds my palm together, the warm blood pouring through my fingers.

The man leaps off the toilet and buries his knife in my chest. He stabs me again, driving me back into the urinal. "No one interrupts the Dark Lord."

He rips out the knife and rabbit punches my chest and stomach, the blade tearing me apart.

I can't breathe. Can't think. Blood everywhere.

The man stands and looks down at me, a flicker of flame behind his eyes. "See you soon, Zach." He flushes the urinal on me and walks away.

The correct choice was to make his friend check on him.

Turn to page 96.

Walking up stairs sounds terrible, and the cops would catch up to me before I get up to the bell.

I face the priest and two cops standing beside him at the back door. "If I die, you're next."

I step up to the statue, a light aura surrounding it. Knowing this is going to hurt, I apologize to Mary and take her off the pedestal, hugging her to my chest with my good forearm, my broken one down by my side.

The statue is probably only forty pounds, but it's red-hot and burning my skin. "Don't follow!"

I doubt they'll listen, or at least not for long, so I hurry out the side door and head for the pond. "Mary," I say as my chest and arms burst into flames. "Pray for me."

EEHHHH! Satan buzzes like it's the wrong answer in a game show. *I'm sorry but the caller you're trying to reach can't help you.*

My face melts as Mary's smile bounces up and down just inches away, a beauty I'll embrace through this hell.

Yeah, I'd fuck her.

"Fuck you!" I shout, leaping for the pond. In the air, I flip onto my back so the statue's above me.

I hit the water hard, and the statue smashes into my jaw, breaking it. I sink to the bottom, keeping my mouth open and sucking in the water. Finally finishing this.

You really think this will end my night? That maybe you saved the world?

It doesn't matter. My body shudders. Game over.

Great. Another terrible ending. Maybe I should have tried:

Go up to the bell tower and find a way to finish this.

Turn to page 102.

Or I could return to the main path and attempt to:

Have sex in order to get the knife from Beth.

Turn to page 16.

Stun her with a headbutt and restrain her.

Turn to page 78.

Or give up and go to the Author Note at the end and find out who Satan's going to fuck with next.

Beth works tomorrow afternoon and will be hurting with a hungover if she drinks any more. Plus, I've got everything I've ever wanted right next to me. There's absolutely no reason to share her with others when we can go home and have sex.

"If you don't mind, I think I'd rather just celebrate with you." I kiss her cheek. "Let's head home."

She squeezes my thigh, her thumb lightly brushing my cock. "Sounds perfect."

My wine glass is still half full. I down it and get up from the table, pull out Beth's chair despite the numerous times she's told me I don't need to do that type of stuff.

"Always the gentleman," she says, smoothing her short black skirt and adjusting her yellow sleeveless silk top over her bra.

Beth leads the way through the restaurant so I can order the ride. I open the front door for us and say, "That way," taking us right on the sidewalk, the opposite direction of The Rusty Knife.

"Should we just walk home?" she asks.

"No way." I wrap my hand around her waist, keeping to her left so I'm closer to the street and the harbor beyond it, six-story buildings lining the block on her side. "We just need to meet the driver at the ride share spot up at the corner."

"Oh good. These heels are hell."

"Take them off. You can wash your feet when we get home."

"Now you're talking." She holds on to me for support as she slips them off.

Without the heels, the top of Beth's head barely reaches my chest. I've always had a soft spot for smaller women. Billy, my boy at The Rusty Knife, swears I "just want my tiny dick to appear bigger," but Billy's also an idiot who says a lot of stupid shit.

We continue down the street, hand in hand until the bench at the corner. "Have a seat." I check my app. "Green Honda Civic. Three minutes."

Beth sits and sets her shoes on the bench beside her. "No limo for your soon-to-be-bride? What a cheapskate."

I chuckle and put my phone away, stepping behind Beth to massage her shoulders.

"Oooohh." She rolls her neck in a slow circle. "Who needs a limo when I have my own masseur?"

"Right?" I work her traps, careful not to squeeze too hard and trigger a headache. This is where she holds so much of her stress. There's nothing better than feeling it melt away under my fingers.

Two guys that look in their fifties are chatting it up as they cross the street, headed our way. Realizing they're not a threat, I turn my focus back on Beth who's admiring her ring.

"God help me!" a man screams.

My hands freeze on Beth's shoulders. That's not someone fucking around. That dude is scared to death. I can't place its source, but it sounds like it's high up in the building behind us.

"Ahhhhhhhhhh!" the man shouts, his scream only getting louder.

I look up and see him plummeting right at us, mouth open, eyes panicked, arms windmilling. I push Beth off the bench and into the street, but there's nowhere for me to go before the collision.

The correct choice was to get a drink at the bar.

Turn to page 72.

"The Number of the Beast" blasts through the speakers as Beth grinds on her pool cue, her blood and beer-soaked body matching the faded red felt of the table. She's surrounded by guys hooting and hollering, a couple digging out phones to capture the memory. I can't fight them all. My only hope is getting Beth down and out of here.

"Beth!" I yell, wanting to pull her off the table but realizing how much it could hurt her. "What the hell are you doing?"

She pulls the stick out from between her legs and jams the thick end into my chest, shoving me back into a big biker. "Fight for me, you fucking loser."

"Yeah, loser," the biker says, his breath reeking of beer and cigarettes.

"Everyone calm down!" I scream, but it's drowned out by the music, cheering, and jeering. There's no more time to talk. The motherfucker to my left throws a huge hook I barely dodge.

Another blow connects right behind my ear and I drop. I cover my head and turn to my side, curl in a ball to absorb the kicks. One of the bastard's steel-toed boots cracks a rib. I roll under the pool table and grimace as I get on all fours on the other side.

Someone's shin slams into my stomach, but it only pisses me off. The guy loads up for another one, but I launch at his locked knee, the snap and scream assuring me I blew it out.

I glance up and see some dick in a backward hat scramble onto the pool table with Beth. Just as I'm getting to my feet, Beth breaks the pool cue against the side of his head. Stunned, he doesn't even try to stop her from jamming the jagged end of the cue in his eye.

The music cuts off and all we hear is this dude screaming on top of the table, the bartender yelling she's calling the cops. I grab Beth's ankle and yell, "Come on!"

Beth slips out of my grip just as someone wrenches my other hand behind my back. They spin me around and run me straight into the dividing counter, crushing my sternum, making it so I can barely breathe.

It's the biker, his breath and scratchy beard giving him away. He grabs the back of my head and aligns my face with the bottle of Coors on the counter in front of me.

I see where this is headed, and scream at him to stop. "Don't do it!"

He kicks out my leg and shoves my head down.

I shout, "No!" but there's no stopping, the bottle knocking out my front teeth and slamming into the back of my throat, the sound of glass breaking.

All I can see is the bottom of Beth's soaked top when she runs up. She raises her arms and shouts, "Fuck this pussy!" Her hands slam down on the back of my head, completely shattering the bottle, the shards shredding my throat.

The biker releases hold of me and I drop to the floor, choking on my blood.

The correct choice was to grab a weapon and fight.

Turn to page 20.

I just pledged my life to this woman less than an hour ago, but I'm not going to sacrifice that life on day one to whatever psychotic breakdown she's in the middle of. Plus, fucking will always trump dying in my book.

I look Beth in her eyes, ignoring the red flicker of flame that must be the reflection of flashing lights on the street. "Yes. Without a doubt, I want to be with you."

"Oh good." She throws herself back onto me, no easing in, so wet there's no need.

I hate how good it feels. "Oh, damn it."

"That's my little bitch," she says, riding me so hard I'm afraid she's going to snap my dick in half. She's got one hand wrapped around my throat, the other holding the knife just a few inches from my eyes.

"Careful," I beg. "Please."

Beth doesn't let up, but turns her head toward the homeless guy. "Wow," she says. "Now that's a cock."

The guy's pants are puddled around his dirty feet, both hands tugging on his dick.

"Bring it over here," she tells him, fucking me so hard I'm about to cum.

The guy grunts and crawls toward us.

"Fuck this," I say, shooting my load into Beth and bucking her forward, throwing her over me. Thick gooey drops rain on my face.

I flip over fast and jump to my feet, careful not to trip. Beth's face down, crying, begging for me to help her.

The homeless dude is stunned, looking like a horse on all fours, his dick dangling.

"Go!" I tell him, kicking him in the ass to hurry him up. I spot the knife next to Beth and grab it, stay back a few feet from her.

"Help me," Beth says, sounding like her old self, just broken and so sad. She turns over, her cheek scratched and lip bleeding. She holds her hand to it and sobs. "Not me, Zach. I can't..."

I pull up my jeans and wipe our fluids off my face, staying right where I am because this has to be some sort of trap. "Are you serious? Are you done?"

She cackles as she stands. "No, you stupid asshole. How gullible are you?" she asks as she wipes her pussy, shaking off the semen. "See wasn't that fun?"

Keeping the knife by my side, I say, "Beth, I don't know what the hell's going on, but we need to get home. You're going to get us arrested."

"Alright," she says, stepping closer.

"Really?"

She launches her knee into my balls before I can turn, the blow doubling me over. "But first you've got to catch me."

I struggle to stand and limp after her down the alley.

She makes a left at the sidewalk, but it takes me a minute to make it to the corner. Beth is waiting for me at the end of the block outside a liquor store. "You going to get me a bottle of whiskey," she shouts, "or do I have to do everything in this relationship?"

I will go in on my own, but get her a non-alcoholic one so she doesn't kill herself.

Turn to page 94.

I need to stop enabling her. I'm telling her I'm headed home, with or without her.

Turn to page 99.

I've had enough and can't take this shit anymore. "I'll get the ring, but you're staying right here," I tell Beth.

"No, you're not," she says, arms crossed. "You're boosting me over first."

"No, Beth," I say, keeping an eye out for cameras or security guards on the other side of the fence. "I'm getting it and I'm keeping it until we figure out what the fuck's wrong with you."

She huffs. "Fine. Think I give a shit? I need a real man, not one afraid of breaking a few rules."

I shake my head. "Yep, that's me," I say, turning my back on her. The fence has two horizontal bars. One to hold onto a foot below the spikes, another a foot or so from the bottom. I step onto the bottom rung with my right foot, and the top with my left, my arms keeping me balanced. I try to make sure Beth is staying put, but I get so wobbly it's not possible. I just have to get over.

This is awkward as hell, and I regret not just boosting her over. My triceps tremble as I hold myself in place, getting the nerve to make the jump. I push off with my right foot and start over the fence.

Beth grabs my ankles and pulls me back, my momentum gone and body falling.

The spikes tear through my stomach, my scream cut short by the intense pain.

"Look at the tough guy now," Beth says with an evil chuckle. "You look more like a shit kabob."

"Help me," I say through tears, using my arms to stop my torso from sinking further.

"No thanks." Beth climbs onto me, dropping all her weight on my lower back, the spikes driving through me.

"Beth..."

"Whee," she says, sliding down and landing on her feet. She kicks the engagement ring into the bushes and strolls toward the church. "Help yourself, loser."

The better choice was to help her over and go out the front parking lot. Turn to page 67.

I've been in enough bar fights and witnessed four times that many to know how quickly shit can go wrong. These motherfuckers aren't looking to discuss this with me.

There's a glass stein half full of beer on the pool table behind me. The guy it belongs to is about to grab it for a drink, but I'm faster and snatch it away from him. The bearded biker rushing me from the left is my biggest threat. I spin and catch the bastard in the side of his head, the stein shattering. Big man's eyes go wide, and his body barrels into the booth Beth and I had been in.

Something slams into the back of my head and sends stars across my vision, but I keep my feet. I turn to the suckerpunching bitch in the Slayer tank top and bullrush him, hands on his ribs. I get underneath his center of gravity, lift him into the air, slam him down on the floor.

Crack!

The end of the pool stick that just broke across my back goes clattering across the room. The dickhead wearing all black holding the sharpened lower half looks shocked the blow didn't do more damage. He almost seems sorry, but before he can change his mind and attack, I rifle a right cross to his mouth, his lips bursting as his lights go out, his head clunking off the tile.

I turn for the next attacker, but everyone else backs off. The rest of these pussies would rather not end up on the ground.

Beth jumps down from the table and wraps me in a huge, sticky hug. "I knew you could do it."

I push her back. "What the fuck's wrong with you?"

"What? I'm not worth fighting over?"

"We're getting out of here," I say, my right hand bleeding, no way of telling if it was from the glass or someone's teeth.

"So, let's go," she says. "This place fucking sucks anyhow."

Beth almost never cusses, at least not around me, but she's never fucked herself with a bottle on one of our dates either. She's already running for the exit, knocking down every bottle and cup on the counter.

Everyone's shouting, the bartender yelling the cops are coming, someone threatening he's going to kill us. I keep running, careful not to slip in the broken glass and liquid.

The out-of-shape security guard is blocking the front door, hand on his holster. He pops off the retention strap as Beth runs right at him. Barely slowing, she kicks him in the nuts and bounces off his body as he doubles over. She grabs hold of his ears and drags him to the ground, jumps on his back like this WWE. "Yeehaw, motherfuckers!" she says, leaping off him and out the door.

I run past the guard, my only concern getting hold of Beth before she hurts herself. Or gets arrested and ruins the rest of her life. I hope they don't have security footage, but even if they don't, someone had to have captured video of us. The second we get home, we're deleting all social media accounts. We're so fucked.

Beth runs down the street, not stopping when I yell her name. At the first alley, she breaks left.

I turn into the dark alley, not able to see or hear her anywhere. "Beth! Beth?" I call out, walking deeper into the darkness between the towering buildings. "Where are you? I want to help."

There's movement to my left, but I'm too slow in turning. Beth slams into my chest, knocking me to the ground. The back of my head bounces off the concrete, but a moment later I open my eyes in disbelief as she straddles me. She's got something sharp pressing against my neck. "Don't move a muscle or I'll slit your fucking throat," she whispers, her breath reeking of beer and sulfur.

I don't know where she got the knife or whatever it is she has to my throat, but I'm smart enough to know I can't trust her not to do something insane.

Her other hand reaches between her legs and unzips my jeans. She grabs hold of my dick, which has never been smaller.

Someone coughs to the side. It's the homeless dude in the cardboard box house beside the trashcan.

"Keep it down," Beth tells him, "or you'll miss the show."

"Beth, what are you doing?"

She squeezes my cock which suddenly isn't half as scared as me. She flashes me the knife, which I'm guessing she took from pool hall, and leans in close. "Having a good time with my fiancée."

This is insane. It won't be my first time fucking in a public place, or in front of an audience, but I've never done anything freaky with Beth. And never due to a death threat.

"You still want to spend the rest of your life with me?" she asks. She puts pressure on my throat. The skin breaks and a bit of blood runs down my neck.

Have sex in order to get the knife from Beth.

Turn to page 16.

Stun her with a headbutt and restrain her.

Turn to page 78.

Knock her forearm across my body and put her to sleep with a head/arm choke.

Turn to page 60.

I let go of Beth's wrist. She won't forgive me if I stop her from saving someone's life. She runs across the street toward the crazy bastard who's lying crumpled in the far lane several yards from the bus. I'm right behind her, but I head for the bus driver who's leaning his shoulder against the railing and sobbing.

"It wasn't your fault," I say. "He went crazy in the bar."

This driver is beyond consoling, so I turn to Beth. She's kneeling on the pavement, cradling the man's misshapen head as blood pours from his torn mouth and forehead, running through her fingers and down her thighs.

The cops are only a few seconds behind us. The chubby male whose nametag reads Gomez tells Beth to get away from purple shirt while his female partner questions the bus driver.

"She's a nurse," I inform Gomez. "And we saw the whole thing."

"Emergency personnel are enroute," he says like a hardass. "Let him go."

A hard shiver rips through Beth, and she makes a noise that makes me think she's about to puke. "He's dead," she says, letting the guy's head smack the ground.

"Hey, hey, hey," I say, shocked by her behavior. I help her up, but she tries walking back across the street. I put my hand on her shoulder. "Hold on."

She turns to me, barefoot and bloody, the bus's flashing hazard lights reflecting red in her eyes. "What?"

"Hey," Gomez says, looking at me. "Don't go far. You'll need to answer questions."

"Sure thing," I say, with zero intention of sticking around. I point at The Knife. "We'll be at the bar."

"Hurry up, slow poke," Beth says, skipping across the street, suddenly careless like a kid in the park.

I hurry after Beth, stopping her right before she reaches the sidewalk and tears her feet up on the shattered glass. "Come on." I guide her around the crowd standing outside. "Let's get you cleaned up."

"Maybe I like being dirty," she says in a dark, seductive voice that doesn't mesh with the blood staining her shirt and dripping down her legs.

I take us left at the corner, wondering how much of her attitude can be attributed to being drunk and the shock of the man dying in her arms.

"Zach! Zach! Hold up!" Billy says, jogging after us.

I let Beth walk ahead so Billy can't see what shape she's in. I wipe my bloody hands onto my jeans and say, "What's up, man?"

"That dude's friend offed himself on the toilet. Slashed the shit out of his forearms."

"Holy shit. This is nuts."

"What the fuck is going on?"

"I wish I knew," I say, realizing Beth is halfway down the street. "Damn, I gotta go."

I catch up to her at the next corner. "Beth! Where are you going?"

She heads down the side street, points to the small neon sign three doors down. All it says is J.C.'s in front of two crossed pool cues. "I need a fucking drink."

I take the giant X of the cues as a sign not to enter. The pounding metal music pulsing through the door doesn't exactly scream date night, and the last thing Beth needs right now is more to drink. "You're covered in blood and your shoes are back there. And shit, where's your purse?"

Beth sucks back a loogie, something she's never done in front of me, and hocks it smack dap in the middle of the sign. "We'll get them later," she says, opening the door and slipping inside before I can stop her.

Other than the lights over each of the pool tables and the neon signs on the walls and above the bar, it's dark as hell in here. I hope it'll keep anyone from noticing us and the shape she's in, but Beth is standing in front of the giant red jukebox beside the door, it's light shining off her bloody arms.

"Put on this one," she tells me, dabbing her finger on the glass, leaving a crimson blot.

"We need to get you cleaned up."

Beth spins on me, shocks me into taking a step back. "It's just a little blood," she says, sucking it off one of her fingers. She turns for the booths besides the pool tables where more than half of the men are watching us. "And get me some alcohol. Chop chop."

She's never ordered me around, not once, and I'm wondering if she got a concussion or maybe someone spiked her drink. Not wanting to make things worse, I check the jukebox, look right below her mark. There are a couple of songs it could be, but I'm pretty sure she picked Iron Maiden's "The Number of the Beast" even though she's never once mentioned liking the band. I put in a five-dollar bill and press its button, along with the two songs above and below it because I'm sure to catch shit if I'm wrong.

When I turn away, Beth has made it into a booth, and it seems like everyone is back to their games and conversations. I head for the bar where an older security guard with a giant belly and a gun holstered on his hip rests against the counter. I can just about guarantee he doesn't have a license to carry in here, but I also can't say I don't blame him considering the crowd. And his body. This guy would have a heart attack five punches into a fist fight.

He nods at me when I walk past. I return the nod to let him know I'm not the kind of guy who'll be any trouble.

The bartender is about as pretty as I'd expect for a place like this, and her caked-on makeup does not help matters. Neither does the scowl she gives when I ask for a pitcher of water.

"Water? You'll have to pay for it."

"No problem. And how about a pitcher of Ultra?"

"Of course," she says, shaking her head like I'm not standing here.

There's a row of men sitting at the counter dividing the bar and the pool tables, and I can barely make out the top of Beth's head. I'm a little surprised no one's approached her yet, but that could definitely be due to her I-just-killed-a-man look.

I pay for the pitchers and ask if there's any way I can get a roll of paper towels.

"Yeah," she says. "At the fucking supermarket."

The security guard snorts as I walk away with a pitcher and stein in each hand. I'd rather not be bringing Beth anything to drink, but I feel like something needs to bring her down a bit; her sudden playfulness has me worried about how she's dealing with everything.

I walk past the line of men sitting at the counter. A couple shoot me looks, but most seem like cowards who only want an easy target. I pass between two of the tables, careful to steer clear of the players, especially the huge biker with the beard and his jacked buddy in the Slayer tank top.

At the booth, I set everything down, just now noticing Beth making a sexy face and moaning in the corner. She's not trying to hide that her hand is busy doing something under the table. And rather aggressively. "Umm. Everything okay?"

"*Ummmmm* is right," she says, sounding and looking like she's about to cum.

I slide into the booth and sit across from her, glancing around to make sure no one's watching. "What are you doing?"

She brings her hand out from below the table, a tabasco bottle clutched hard. She sets it down besides the pitchers. "Oh, so spicy. Muy caliente."

The top half of the bottle glistens. I'm speechless.

She pushes it across the table. "Your turn."

Holy shit. She's snapped.

I tell her, "We need to leave."

"Go ahead."

"Together. I'm not leaving you here."

"Then get comfy, motherfucker," she says with an evil grin.

What the hell? The plan was to get all that blood washed off her, but there's no way I'm letting her out of my sight to go to the bathroom. I doubt she'd go anyway. "Can you at least get cleaned up?" I ask, pushing forward the water.

"Fine," she says, "since you're such a little baby. But beer first."

I grab a handful of napkins and dab them in the water, cleaning off my forearms. Beth picks up the pitcher but doesn't bother using the stein, just puts it to her lips and chugs. Beer spills all over her, running down her throat and soaking her blouse, her nipples clearly hard.

Beth slams down the empty pitcher. "How's that?" she asks with a twisted smile.

"It was—"

Buurrrppppp!

That burp is louder than I can muster, and half the patrons are staring. "Jesus, Beth."

"Do not use that name!" she shrieks, the muscles sticking out in her neck, pure fury on her face.

Oh my God. If people hadn't been looking, they sure as hell are now.

I get out of the booth, not sure what I'm going to do. I need help, but I'm not going to get it from any of the scumbags filling this place.

I pull out my phone to see if there are any emergency psychiatric services I can call. I walk a few feet from the booth, but my service sucks in here.

The intro to "The Number of the Beast" begins. Beth says, "This is my jam."

I hurry over to the bar. "Excuse me," I say, trying to get the bartender's attention. "I need help for my girlfriend, but don't know who to call."

"You mean her?"

Beth is dancing on the pool table next to our booth, treating the pool stick like it's her broom and she's in the middle of furious game of Quidditch.

Everyone hurries toward her table, cheering her on. I run over, pushing people out of the way, yelling at Beth to get down.

She looks at me then back at the crowd of men surrounding her. "Whoever beats up this pussy," she says, pointing at me before putting both hands on the pool cue tight to her crotch, "can beat up this pussy."

Grab the closest weapon because shit is about to get real.

Turn to page 20.

There are too many men to fight. I have to de-escalate the situation.

Turn to page 14.

I'm seriously considering choking Beth back out, but that would only be a temporary fix. She needs real help. As crazy as it sounds, especially since I never believed in the guy, I think she needs Jesus in her life. Pronto.

"Move," I say, pushing her forward, keeping my grip on the sheet because she'll bolt the second I let go.

"Such a little momma's boy."

"Just move." I push her forward, not giving her a chance to do anything but walk. Fortunately, there have only been a few cars driving on this street and no one seems to have paid us any attention.

Beth gets excited when we pass the liquor store on the corner. "Oh, please, please, please, get me a bottle.

"Are you crazy? I'm not getting you anything else to drink."

"I'll suck your dick."

"Keep moving," I say.

As we cross the street, I try to block the image of her biting my cock off. At the next corner, we make a left, the entrance to St. Mark's parking lot halfway down the block. The moon shining off the silver bell in the rooftop tower fills me with hope. I know this is stupid and probably won't help, but I've got nothing else to hold on to.

"Why didn't you say where we were going?" she says, picking up speed.

"You're happy about this?"

She keeps walking, turning left into the parking lot without me redirecting her.

The church is off to our right. On the left are two small houses, a wooden bridge and a little pond separating them. I'm not positive which one the priests live in, but I'm guessing it's the first one with the lights on in the back rooms. As we get closer, I see the sign pointing at it: Rectory.

It's not until we're about to walk up the stairs to the small porch that I question why she's stopped fighting me. "Beth? You there?"

She turns her head toward me and for a second, I'm sure she's going to keep spinning it all the way around. "Yeah, just going where you said. I'm a good little girl who only wants to obey," she says with a dark, childish laugh. A flicker of flame dances in her eyes.

I walk her up the stairs, steering her to the side with the bench and planter filled with white roses since she seems to want to be here and I'd rather not have her be the first thing they see when they open up. I knock on the door.

"Oh, I love these," she says.

I think she's talking about the flowers and not the Ring doorbell I'd missed. She has her right leg raised, her dirty foot resting on the wall right above it, her skirt falling back to show she lost her panties along the way.

"Hello," an irritated man says through the doorbell. "It's past ten o'clock. Who is this?"

"Check the camera," she says, laughing as she lets loose a stream of piss.

I push Beth away from the drenched Ring, forgetting she's balanced on only one leg. She falls and crashes into the wooden bench. With her arms tied to her sides, her head bounces off the edge and she collapses to the porch, lights out.

Heavy footsteps approach the door. The dead bolt clicks. The door opens an inch, just enough for an older white man to peer through. "What do you want?"

"Help. For my fiancé."

"What's wrong with her?"

"Everything," I say, about to breakdown crying.

The man, who's wearing blue sweatpants and a white T-shirt, steps back and opens the door. "Where is she?"

I point to the side where Beth is groaning, opening her eyes. "She's gone crazy," I tell him.

The man steps onto the porch and gasps. "She needs a hospital," he says, looking like he's about to run inside and call the cops on me.

"No. That's not her blood. Mostly."

"Why is she tied up?"

"She needs Jesus."

"What?"

"She's possessed. I know that doesn't make any sense, but she said so herself."

Beth rolls into a sitting position. Propping herself up, she turns to us and spreads her legs. "Let him decide for himself," she says. "If I taste evil then Satan's inside me. But if I taste better than Miss Tabitha's rotten roast beef sandwich, Father Paul will know you're lying."

I hurry in front of her as the man's face goes even whiter. She hit the bullseye. Satan knows his shit.

Unable to look at Father Paul, I help Beth to her feet. "This isn't her. Look at her eyes."

A middle-aged man in plaid pajamas runs out from the rectory, eyes wide. A guy with a crewcut who looks about my age is right behind him and asks, "What's happening?"

"I promise you," she tells Father Paul, her breath reeking of sulfur, "I fuck way harder than she can. And I won't make you feel so guilty about the strap-on."

"Gag her," he orders. "Now."

"Oh, gag me, Daddy, with that big ole cock," she says, making me want to swear this isn't my fiancée, that she'd never in a million years talk like this.

I don't have any way to shut her up, and there's no way in Hell I'm putting my hands near her mouth. The chubby guy in plaid pajamas runs into the building and comes right back with a black scarf.

"Uh oh. Father James B. Butt-Fucker means business."

The priest is furious. He wraps the scarf around Beth's head, pulling tight and tying it off.

"Careful," I tell them as we walk her inside. "He wanted to come here. Don't trust him for a second."

"Stop misgendering me, Zach," she says around the gag which isn't doing much good. "Five more years in the pit of suffering for the verbal assault."

We're in a small lobby. No one sits behind the receptionist's desk, but a nameplate between a phone and inbox reads 'Tabitha Wheeler.'

Father Paul steps in front of the sign and points to the hallway. "Get her in that first bedroom. On the bed."

Beth jumps up and down so excited, and spits out the scarf she just chewed through. "Oh yes, oh yes," she says, in the little kid voice. "To be fucked by the hand of God."

I rush Beth to the bed, it's white sheet about to be ruined. I push her onto it and flip her over so she's facing the ceiling fan. I sit on her hips to stop her flopping around, but that doesn't prevent her from slamming her knees into my back.

"What are you doing?" I shout at the priests just standing there staring. "Grab her goddamn legs."

The small guy with the buzz cut grabs hold of her ankles and leans back, keeping her lower half still.

Father Paul runs into the room with a rosary and a crucifix. "We must perform an exorcism!"

"We can't," Father James says. "The Bishop will have our heads if we don't have written approval."

"You want to call him and put in the request?" Father Paul asks.

The priest holding her ankles says, "She needs to be examined. Medical and psychological."

Beth thrusts me up her hips and opens her knees. "Examine this, Father Luke the Licker."

"How does she know our names?" Luke asks.

I can't handle this shit. "Because she has a fucking demon in her! Just save her. I'm begging."

"I'll take responsibility," Father Paul says. "We must try."

"You ever done one?" Luke asks.

"Of course not, but do you have a better idea?"

"So what do we do?" Father James asks, sounding pretty damned scared.

"I think you stuff the cross in my naughty hole," Beth says.

"Alexa," Father Paul says. "How do you perform an exorcism?"

Beth can't stop laughing. "Oh shit. You guys are so fucked."

Alexa suggests a list of prayers and psalms, almost none of which I recognize. All my attention is on Beth and the growing dance of flames in her eyes. Her sick smile shows Satan's enjoying every second of this.

"James, get the holy water," Paul says.

The pajama priest runs out of the room as Beth calls him a good boy. "And bring me back a bone. A huge, throbbing, pink one."

Father Paul steps along the side of the bed closest to the wooden-framed window, his crucifix held in front of him aimed at Beth. "God of Heaven, God of Earth, God of the angels, God of archangels—"

"God of holy fucking repetitive shit," Beth shouts over him.

Paul keeps talking, saying something about the forces of darkness. He brings the crucifix closer to Beth, and she pushes back into the bed, her first sign of weakness.

Father James rushes back into the room and takes his place to my left, a bottle of Evian in hand. When Paul stares at him, James unscrews the cap and says, "I blessed it."

"Bless this, you stupid fucks!" Beth shouts before she sinks her teeth into her lower lip and spits the blood at my face.

Paul looks behind me. "Luke, do not let her go. Recite St. Michael the Archangel's prayer."

Father Luke launches into prayer, and Beth kicks her legs in futility, panic showing beneath the fury.

Father Paul makes a sign of the cross with his rosary and lowers the crucifix so it's only a foot from a gnashing Beth, the tendons in her neck fully flexed. "What is your name?" he demands.

"My name is..." Beth stills her body as sweat rolls off her forehead. "My name is..." Looking him in the eyes, she smiles. "My name is Slim Shady."

"Demon! I command you in the name of Jesus Christ. What is your name?"

"Oh me," Beth says, back in the innocent little girl voice. "I'm Beth Angel Lattimer."

Paul looks to James and tells him, "Repeat my words and sprinkle her with the water."

"Fuck that," Beth says to James. "Say your own words and sprinkle me with your sweet cum."

I want to disappear, to wake a million miles from here, but there's no escape. Father Paul has already launched into his prayer, James right behind him.

"I adjure you, ancient serpent, by the judge of the living and..."

"Ow! You asshole!" Beth yells as the first drops of water hit her flesh. They each evaporate in a puff of smoke, leaving a ring of blackened skin in their wake.

Father Paul orders James to keep going, and continues the prayer, demanding the demon depart from this servant of God.

"Boring!" Beth says, grimacing at the holy water but trying to hide her pain.

Paul touches the crucifix next to the purple bruise on Beth's forehead and her skin sizzles. She screams as he says, "In the name of Jesus Christ."

Beth drives the crucifix out of the way and nearly bites Paul's thumb.

Paul is unfazed, looking like his anger is keeping him in control. "I command you, unclean spirit, to leave this servant of God," he says, pushing the crucifix onto Beth's chest.

She thrashes around as smoke billows off her.

"Come Holy Spirit," James says, sprinkling his water on Beth's face as Father Paul repeats his command. "Fill me with Your love, peace, and strength."

"No!" Beth's flesh burns as she bucks her hips and bangs the top of her head into the headboard. "Leave me," she says, sounding exactly like herself. Like a switch was flipped, she goes silent, her body limp on the bed.

Father Paul pulls the crucifix back and James stops his sprinkling. Paul says, "In the name of Jesus Christ, and by the power..."

Beth's eyes flutter open, tears flowing. "Zach, make them stop," she says, gasping for air, her eyes slits so I can't tell if there are any flames. "He's gone, but it hurts. I can't breathe."

The priests continue their verbal assault, but their words aren't triggering her.

"Zach, please. I'm begging you," she says, so weak, her face tinting blue. "Get off."

We have to finish this.

Turn to page 43.

They're hurting Beth and need to stop.

Turn to page 5.

I glance over my shoulder out the window, afraid none of the priests or nuns look like heroes who would risk their lives for Beth. I've already ruined her life. I won't end it.

"Answer me!" Satan shouts, my throat scraped raw.

Before he can force me forward, I tear off my shirt, wrap it around my hand. The second it touches the stove, it goes up in a beautiful ball of flames. *Church!* I tell Satan.

Fine, you figure it out, Satan says, letting me feel all the pain.

Each step is hell as I hurry out the backdoor, limping as fast as my leg will allow. My hand is cooking. I want to run to the pond and put out the fire, but I know that Satan won't allow anything but me heading to the church. It isn't much farther. The church's back door is so close, only ten yards away.

I hit the wooden door hard and try the handle with my left hand. It's fucking locked. The door is old walnut, the frame peeling. I hold my burning hand to it, the wood catching.

Satan pulls my arm back and squats down, holding the flame under my ass, frying my jeans. *Nice try. You gotta burn the inside.*

"It's locked," I cry, forcing my flaming arm away from me, holding it high so it doesn't torch the rest of me.

Tough shit. You made your decision.

Two cop cars pull into the parking lot, their headlights illuminating me, reflecting off the tall stained-glass windows.

That's it. I hobble to the first window, ignoring the screaming priests.

I keep my flaming hand on the wall for support and punch the middle of the window, causing a giant crack.

The cops are out of their cars, yelling at me to freeze.

I punch at the middle of the crack, making it bigger. I punch it again and again. It shatters and slices my forearm open as all but the top of the pane crashes down.

"It's Satan!" Father Paul shouts. "Shoot him!"

"Freeze!" the cops keep yelling, running at me, guns drawn.

Not caring about the pain, I grab hold of the frame and pull myself through the window. A chunk of burning shirt falls from my melting hand and smolders on the carpet.

Someone grabs hold of my right ankle. "Get your ass out here," the cop shouts as another pair of hands grabs hold of my left.

Don't stop now, you pussy, Satan tells me.

The cops pull me back, the jagged bottom of the window frame slicing open my stomach and chest. Just my head remains inside the church.

I glance up at the dangling pane of glass above. "Fuck you, Satan," I say, pounding my shredded fist on the frame.

Satan sees what I'm trying to do and retakes control, but I get in another hit, knocking the glass loose. It falls so fast, I'm not aware what happened until my head stops rolling, propped against the wooden pew.

Satan sticks out my tongue, catching drops of the bloody waterfall pumping out my neck. As my vision fades, he thinks, *See you soon, sucker.*

The better choice might have been to burn down the rectory and risk killing Beth. Turn to page 40.

Or you can go back to the main branch and try to:

Have sex in order to get the knife from Beth. Turn to page 16.

Knock her forearm across my body and put her to sleep with a head/arm choke. Turn to page 60.

Or give up and go to the Author Note at the end and find out who Satan's going to fuck with next.

"You're drunk," I remind Beth, pulling her back into a hug. "Let the cops handle it, babe. Please."

She can't break her gaze from the scene. "My duty."

"Not tonight." I put myself between her and the accident. "You always care for everyone else. Let me do *my* duty and care of you."

Her face lightens and she nods. "You're right. Not my responsibility."

"Let's go back inside." I want to get away from all the shouts and a new bout of sirens. "Hold on. Where are your shoes?"

She turns back to The Rusty Knife and I follow, keeping hold of her hand in case she's being sneaky. This is the drunkest I've seen her, and she detests anyone telling her what she can or can't do.

Fortunately, Beth keeps walking forward, her sway same as mine. Her heels are beside the front door Hans is guarding. We walk around everyone gawking at the disaster from the sidewalk, and I help steady Beth as she slips on her shoes.

When I try to head back inside the bar, Hans stops us. "I'm afraid we're closed."

"They're cool," Billy says from behind the bar.

Hans lets us by and we each take a stool.

"Holy shit." Billy sets three shots on the counter and motions for us to grab ours. "Can this night getting any fucking crazier?"

We down the drinks, the heat only making me feel worse. This was such a terrible idea. "We should get the hell out of here," I tell Beth who keeps looking over her shoulder trying to see what's happening outside.

"Let me through," some rough-sounding dude says from behind.

"Yes, sir," Hans says.

It's the male cop and his female partner that responded to the accident. I'm expecting them to start asking questions, but the guy walks right up beside me and orders a bottle of vodka.

"Excuse me?" Billy says. "You want a drink?"

The cop unholsters his gun and places it on the bar, the barrel pointed at Billy's stomach, his finger on the trigger. "I stutter, you stupid fuck?"

"Woah, woah, woah," Billy says, backing up, the bottles shaking in their display when he bumps into it. He grabs a vodka bottle and side-eyes me to ask what the hell is going on, before he sets it in front of the cop.

"Gomez," the female cop says from right behind me. "What are you doing?"

"What's with all the dumb fucking questions?" Gomez picks up the bottle in his free hand. He raises it to his lips and takes a five-second chug, somehow keeping it down.

"Gomez," the female says, much sterner. "Take your hand off your pistol."

"Nah, bitch," he says, spinning around, the barrel of his gun grazing my shoulder.

"What are you doing?" she screams.

Blam! Blam!

My hearing is gone, the gun going off inches from my ear. I recoil and slip off the stool, knocking Beth off hers.

Gomez spins toward Billy and fires one shot. "And another one bites the dust," he sings with a chuckle.

I cover Beth, looking over my shoulder at Gomez who has the gun aimed at my face, a flicker of flame behind his soulless black eyes. I hold up my hand. "Wait! What are you—"

Blam!

The correct choice was to let Beth help.

Turn to page 23.

Choosing between self-immolation and killing my fiancée isn't much of a choice, especially when I can't trust Satan's word and that he'll even abide by my decision.

Now you're thinking, Fucko. Still gotta choose though.

"Fine." I grab the dishtowel off the oven handle and hold it to the flames. The towel catches fire fast. I turn and hobble to the window, set both curtains blazing bright. "The rectory. There."

"There, my ass," Satan says, taking control, suppressing the pain flowing through me. "I said the rectory, not some tiny bullshit curtains."

The flames are licking the ceiling. *It's burning! Look!*

"Not nearly enough." He walks me down the hallway, the bone-on-bone grind of my shattered shin killing me with each step. The dishtowel is burning my hand, but he acts as if everything's rosy, humming an upbeat "Walking on Sunshine" as we approach Beth's room.

No, no, no. Leave her alone.

From the tiny bedroom's doorway, Satan stares at Beth passed out on the bed, angry burn marks dotting her face and arms. "One, you don't tell me what to do. And two," he says, tossing the burning towel at the foot of the bed, "fuck you."

The bottom of the sheet catches fire. Somehow, I find my voice and shout, "Help! She's burning!"

"Oh, you little shit." Satan pushes off on my good leg and jumps straight up, staring down so I witness all my weight about to land on my broken one.

I hit the ground hard. With a sickening snap like a breaking sapling, the lower half of my shin rips through my skin, pushes against my jeans. Even with the pain buried along with me, it's still excruciating. *Oh fuck. Stop the pain. Stop this! I'm sorry!*

Satan crawls me back toward the kitchen, intentionally dragging my shin on the carpet.

Headlights pour through the windows as the cop cars pull up to the building, sirens blaring.

Flames cover the kitchen ceiling, the heat unbearable as Satan crawls to the stove. He grabs hold of the red-hot edge just inches from the burners to pull myself up, my fingers blistering. Once I'm standing, my head cooking, the air hard to breathe, I grab the bottle of whiskey and set it in the middle of all four flames. "Time for a quick science experiment."

The front door bangs open and someone runs into the hallway. It's a police officer holding a rag over his mouth to deal with the smoke billowing out of Beth's room.

"You here to watch?" Satan asks him. He grabs the aluminum can of cooking spray from the counter and set it in front of the whiskey bottle because he realized this shit's going to take too long.

Satan bends me down so I don't broil my brain yet and miss the ending. My face is less than a foot from the spray can.

The cop draws his gun, aims at me, but peeks into Beth's room.

"Let's play a guessing game," Satan says, coughing on the smoke, my cheek really cooking. "How long do I have?"

"Leave the building!" The cop steps toward me, gun aimed at my head. "I need help!" he shouts over his shoulder. "Her bed's on fire!"

I turn toward the aluminum can, dreading how awful this is going to feel.

Beth screams and I just want this to end.

Boom!

The explosion knocks me back and onto my ass. I can't see out my left eye. A river of blood runs over my right one. I reach up above it. A thin strip of aluminum splits that eyebrow in half.

Satan reaches down and pats the front of my flaming shirt, points out each sliver of shrapnel that's pierced my chest. "And don't forget about this," he says, sounding like shit as he flicks the one lodged in the middle of my throat.

Satan can barely talk with me dying, coughing on the smoke, Beth screaming so loud. "Come on in," he calls to the cop who's backed up to the lobby. "Don't be scared."

The cop flees and Satan smiles. *Alright, Zachie boy, looks like fun time is over. Remember, this is just a tiny taste.*

My entire body is burning, my skin melting as Beth continues to scream.

And it only gets worse from here. For all fucking eternity.

Well, that sucked. Maybe I should have tried to:

Light myself on fire and torch the church.

Turn to page 36.

Or I can return to the main branch and:

Have sex in order to get the knife from Beth.

Turn to page 16.

Knock her forearm across my body and put her to sleep with a head/arm choke.

Turn to page 60.

Or give up and go to the Author Note at the end and find out who Satan's going to fuck with next.

This might really be Beth, but we must be sure. I've already hurt her so much today. A few more minutes isn't going to make a difference.

I look her in the eyes, catching flames flickering. "I'm sorry, babe. Just a little longer."

"Let me go!" she roars, the tendons in her neck bulging.

"We need you," Father Paul tells me, holding out his hand with a rosary wrapped around it.

I don't question him and take hold, his strength surging through me. Father James clutches my other hand. A united front.

Beth screams like she's being murdered. "Fuck you!" she shouts, directing it at me.

"No!" I yell back, hating this motherfucker more than I've ever hated anyone or anything in my entire life. "Fuck you, Satan. You listen to us."

Father Paul lowers the crucifix, aiming the top at Beth's face so she can't snap at him. "Everyone, repeat after me."

Beth keeps screaming as James sprinkles her with the water, her flesh sizzling with each drop.

Father Paul says, "In the name of Jesus Christ," and we repeat his words.

"And by the power of His Cross and Blood."

Beth froths at the mouth, her shouts so guttural I can barely make out the obscenities.

"I take authority over all spirits that are not of the Holy Spirit," we repeat after Paul.

A thought hits me so hard, it has to be a truth. I have to say the most powerful words I can, the sign of true faith. Meaning it with all my heart, and holding onto the priests for strength, I stare at Satan and say, "I hand my life over to Jesus."

Beth shutters violently, and an insane blast of energy knocks me off her. I'm so dizzy I can't stop myself from falling off the bed. My head smacks the wall beside Father James, and I lie crumpled on the floor.

It feels like a dream, Father Paul's voice floating above me. "Cover her with a blanket. The poor child's shivering."

I roll onto my back, let out a long groan.

"James, see to him," Paul says. "He hit his head hard."

It's not easy, but I open my eyes, anxious to get up and hold Beth. I must be bleeding from my forehead because I see everything through a red veil as Father James bends over me with his half-full bottle of water close to spilling. I wipe at my eyes, but the red doesn't go away.

Satan laughs from deep inside me. *Uh oh, Spaghetti-O's,* his voice bellows in my brain.

"No! Get out of me!" I scream. "Leave me!"

Father Paul runs over, stands by my feet. "He's jumped hosts!"

"Help me," I beg them.

Father Paul holds up the crucifix and invokes Jesus Christ, the name filling me with an uncontrollable rage, like the time those three motherfucking seniors stuffed my freshman ass in the trashcan. Father James must notice it because he's tipped the bottle, its contents falling for my face.

I throw my arms up as a shield, the water burning like acid. I flip onto all fours as smoke billows from my forearms, the pain fueling my hatred, Satan in control. I want to warn them, to shout, but I'm being shoved further and further into a corner of my mind, like I'm becoming an unwilling observer who can't close his eyes.

Father James is out of water and trapped in the corner just a few feet from me, praying to Jesus which is only going to make things worse for him.

Satan bunches me up in a 4-point stance like I'm on the defensive line for a goal line stand. I blast forward into James's skinny legs, laughing at the man's pained screams as he falls to the floor.

Father Paul and Luke stand side by side at the foot of the bed like they can stop me. Paul grips the crucifix, their prayers creating a white aura around them Satan wants to avoid.

Son of a bitch, Satan thinks, my heart racing like he's actually afraid.

I want to shout that it's working, for them to close in and trap me, but Satan leaps onto the bed, not caring he just smashed Beth's forearm. He throws us at the window, hitting it with my shoulder. The glass shatters, but the wooden frame only cracks along with my collarbone.

"Stop, Satan! Leave this servant of God!" Paul shouts.

Satan picks me up off the floor, along with a shard of glass. He holds it to my throat. "You really want me to release this punk?" he asks, completely taking over me, my voice so deep, the scent of sulfur making me sick. "Let's do it." He breaks the skin, warm blood dripping down the glass and onto my fist. "Let's see which of your pathetic asses I decide to infiltrate next. Oh, this is going to be so much fun."

"Call the cops," Paul says, pushing Luke out of the bedroom. He grabs hold of James and drags the wailing priest down the hall.

"See. Total pussies." Satan lowers the glass, but keeps it in his hand as he turns to the bed. Beth is passed out, her face and arms covered in burn marks. He takes a step toward her.

No! I won't let him hurt her. I put every ounce of my being into resisting him. "Don't you dare," I say, surprised it worked and I'm back in control. I drop the glass and run into the hallway.

I skid to a halt on no will of my own. "Nice try, fucko," Satan says. He moves me in front of the framed photo of the church packed with parishioners and headbutts it. The glass cracks and the frame falls to the floor. "Cooperate and make it easier on yourself."

Satan glances both directions to confirm the priests have fled. "Dang it. No one wants to play."

I'm surprised at how cool and calm Satan sounds in my head. I was picturing more of a Slayer vibe, but he reminds me an awful lot like the singer from Lord of the Lost.

"I love those guys," Satan says like we're besties, reading my goddamn thoughts. "Really? You're just now getting that? You're mine, Zachie boy. Every damn part. Your body, your thoughts, and if you're a pussy, which you're most definitely turning out to be, your will."

I can't speak the words because he's not lying about the physical control. I think as loud as I can, *I give myself to Jesus.*

Satan laughs out loud, the sulfur stench nauseating. "Sorry, little homie. You ain't a priest and your prayers are nothing more than the desperate pleas of a dead man. Right about now, you'd worship my left testicle if you thought it'd increase your chances of escaping eternal damnation."

I GIVE MY LIFE TO JESUS!

"Alright, that's enough of this stupid shit." He turns me left, walks toward the small kitchen.

I put everything I have into stopping him, but all it does is drag my right foot just a bit.

"Fine. Be difficult," he says, jumping into a kickboxing stance, right leg cocked back.

He makes me look down at the concrete corner of the wall I'm about to blast with my shin. Oh fuck. I used to mess around by kicking wooden objects to toughen up my legs for kickboxing, but that was for six months, and never concrete or at full speed. He's set me up so I'm hitting the corner at the worst possible angle.

"Tough shit," he says, launching my leg at the wall, holding nothing back.

The snap of my shin is nearly as sickening as the wave of pain. I can't do this. I give in.

"That's what I fucking thought," he says, limping me into the small kitchen, each step adding to my hell. I hope he'll take me out the back door, but instead he turns to the window and points out the three women huddled together with the Paul and Luke while James lies on the grass beside them. "Damn it," he says. "Had you played along, we could've had one hell of an orgy."

I stay hidden in the background, too afraid to resist, to feel the pain pouring through me as he shuffles to the cupboard above the fridge. There's a barely touched liter of whiskey. I take it down and spin off the cap, grateful to have something to take the edge off this agony.

"Say goodbye to more than your pain," Satan says as I put the bottle to my lips.

As the whiskey fills my mouth, I remember how desperately Beth needed to drink. I close off my throat, only a small amount getting through.

Satan keeps going, the whiskey overflowing from my mouth and soaking my shirt. With my free hand, he pinches my nose closed and tilts my head back.

I need air and spit the whiskey out around the bottle, unable to stop the rest from flooding my throat. I swallow as fast as possible so I don't drown.

I finish all but an inch and set the bottle beside the stove.

There is no more him and me. He is me. I am him. The one and only motherfucking Satan.

"Goddamn," I say like a drunk cowboy with razor blades lining my throat. "It's time to party."

I turn on all four of the stove's dials. *Click, click, click.* Flames appear. They're so bright and beautiful, warming me up and matching the fuzzy feeling in my stomach.

All a sudden, his happiness sours. We're separate again, Satan still firmly behind the wheel. "Humans are so fucking pathetic," he says. "This isn't a victory to celebrate. How about we play a fun game, Zachie boy? I'm going to let you make the next decision."

A small sense of control returns to me, the pain even more intense.

"What do you want to burn down?" Satan asks. "The rectory and possibly your fiancée or yourself and the church? *If* you can even make it that far."

The sirens are getting closer, but they sound like cops, not firefighters. And the priests and nuns are out there talking all in a panic, little chance they'd rush into a burning building.

What's it gonna be? Tick tock, you little cock.

Maybe if I shout, they'll run in and rescue her before the fire spreads.

Five. Four.

Satan steps me closer to the flame, my shirt heating up.

"Hold on!" I shout.

Two. One!

Light myself on fire and torch the church.

Turn to page 36.

Burn down the rectory and risk killing Beth.

Turn to page 40.

I stare at Beth through the flickering veil of red, anger and sadness filling me. Memories flash of our first date, the night we slept on the beach, the weekend in Big Bear. I'm not throwing her in the dumpster. I failed her in every way possible. I'm not treating her like trash.

"So you'll leave her piled up next to it so some homeless dude can fuck her cooling corpse?" Satan says through my mouth, his words sickening me.

"Fuck you!" I say, taking back control of my voice.

Don't get all jelly. He chuckles, forces me to stare down at Beth, her intestines piled on her lap. *Just trying to help you make the smart move.*

There are no smart moves to make. Everything's so fucked. Tears pour down my face.

Really? he says, sounding so disappointed. *Stop being such a little bitch.*

I slam my fist into the dumpster. The pain gives me clarity and momentarily lowers the red curtain. I run down the alley, breaking right on the sidewalk, no idea where I'm headed, my arms pumping. The light up ahead just turned red but I'm not going to stop.

I'm about to fly past the light post when Satan thinks, *Not so fast, sucker.*

He launches me at the pole, my feet leaving the ground. I hit it with a sickening crunch, my collarbone shattered. I bounce off it, tumble to the concrete.

"Fuck!" I scream, writhing on the ground. I try getting up but can't put any weight on my left arm.

The curtain comes back up, everything red, the excruciating pain now a dull ache buried along with me. Satan forces me to my feet. "I'm in charge, Zachie. Accept that and do my will," he says while waving at the couple in the Prius who just pulled over.

The older blonde in the passenger seat lowers her window. "Oh my gosh. Are you okay?"

"Never better," he tells her. "Off to fuck a pack of virgins to top the night off."

She gasps and the driver punches the gas.

What the hell is wrong with you?

"Long story, little buddy." He walks me across the street, not even turning his head to see if any cars are coming. "But you're in luck and are about to have all of eternity to listen to it."

Nothing you said should send me to Hell.

Cars honk and slam on brakes, but he doesn't bother looking. "Killing your fiancée seems like a fairly good reason. Leaving her to be molested in an alley a close second."

I didn't have a choice.

"Broken record," he says with a yawn.

Satan's walking me back toward the harbor and all the trouble we caused. The sign for JC's pool hall is just ahead. A group of men gather around a contractor's work truck on the opposite side of the street. *What are you doing?*

"I thought it'd be nice to check on your friends, see if they'd like another shot at the champ."

Are you crazy? My left arm's useless and there's four of them.

"Guess it's time to toughen up," he says, crossing the street and heading toward the group. "And who knows, maybe they'll forgive you. Let's see, shall we?"

"Hey, look!" the guy in the leather jacket shouts, pointing right at me. "It's him!"

Oh fuck. The big guy just grabbed a crowbar from the truck. The jacked guy in the Slayer tank top that I had slammed to the pool hall's floor pulls out a two-foot-long metal pipe and smacks it into his palm. I don't see what the bald guy grabs because I concentrate all my energy and force myself to bend over and pick up the chunk of broken brick in the gutter.

Satan regains control, not happy with my detour. "Hey, boys," he says, waving my left hand, the grind of my broken clavicle making me sick.

"You motherfucker," leather jacket says, headed my way. His boys follow right behind. "You're gonna pay."

"Oh, sounds scary," Satan says. He holds out my hand. "Look, I'm almost shaking."

"Fuck this guy," the big guy says, circling to my right.

Leather jacket circles to my left. "You're fucking dead."

You're going to get me killed.

Satan stands perfectly still. "Probably. But at least it's likely one of these guys is going to be a lot less of a pussy than you."

The Slayer guy looks confused for a second, but shakes it off and is first to strike, his metal pipe crushing my left elbow.

I try to move, to swing back, but Satan's locked me out and won't move a muscle.

Big man has his crowbar pulled back and about to swing.

Give me control! I'll serve you!

The veil goes dark red, but I have control of my body, all the pain pouring in. I leap forward and smash the brick into the side of the big man's head, getting to him just a second before his crowbar would have hit. He drops to the street, the crowbar clattering beside him.

Something hard and heavy slams into the back of my head and I stumble forward, smash against the side of the truck. I'm so dizzy, but I spin around and throw the brick at Slayer who's rushing me, shouting something. The brick hits him in the mouth and drops him hard.

The bald guy leaps in front of me, jams his shovel at my chest, the sharp tip tearing my shirt and slicing me open. He jabs me again, pushes me back into the truck. I hear the other guy swinging, but close my eyes before the pipe smashes into my mouth, dropping me to my knees. I spit out so much blood and broken teeth, my brain barely working.

Uh-oh, Zachie. Looks like you fucked up. Shoulda zigged, not zagged.

A blow hits the top of my head, my skull indenting like the first crack in a hard-boiled egg. The shovel slams down on my right hand, two of my fingers detached like bloody sausages as my vision goes dark. Metal collides with my skull and sends me face down, unable to move, the crack so much bigger, my brain leaking from its shell.

The correct choice was to hide Beth's body in the dumpster.
Turn to page 53.

I'll never forgive myself for this, but I swear I'll find a way to make amends. Even if it means rotting in prison for a crime I never wanted to commit. But I can't do anything with this bastard in control.

"Now you're getting it," he says through my mouth. "Hurry up and dump this bitch."

I bend down and cradle Beth in my arms. I kiss her forehead and pick her up, and I find myself thinking she's so heavy as dead weight.

"Ha! Good one," Satan says as I balance her on the edge of the dumpster. The smell from inside is revolting.

I hate myself when I toss her over. She lands with a thud, and a cloud of flies rises up and settles back down, exploring her body. "At least she's not alone," he says as I puke up dinner, the alcohol burning my throat on the way out.

"Really?" He uses my forearm to wipe the splatter of my face. "You know how hard it is to get nuns horny when smelling like crap?"

"You're not doing shit," I say, struggling to get out the words.

"No, no, my friend. I am doing tons of shit. The only question is if you'll be my vessel."

You killed Beth. I'm not helping you. My left legs drags because I'm fighting him from walking down the alley.

He keeps limping, turns left on the sidewalk. "Yeah, this isn't drawing any attention to you."

I don't care. I'm not helping you another step.

Satan fixes his gait. "You know what you need, Zachie?"

You getting the fuck out of me.

"Good guess, but I was thinking more along the lines of a drink," he says, hurrying toward the liquor store on the corner.

I force myself to stop outside the door, catching my reflection in the glass. I spot the flicker of flame in my pupils.

A giant smile spreads across my face. "Nice touch," he says. "Right?"

Leave me!

"Naw, not yet," he says, opening the door to the liquor store.

The clerk, an old guy with a bushy gray beard, is tripping on me, probably hoping he's safe behind his counter with the bulletproof glass barrier. "Woah, woah, woah," he says when I walk past him.

I grab the nearest bottle of whiskey and slam it on the counter. "Don't judge me, Walid, and I won't judge you."

"How you know my name?" he says, looking down at his chest like maybe a nametag magically appeared.

I pull out my last two twenties and push them through the opening under the glass divider. "Name's easy," Satan says. "Knowing you're wanted for murder back home is a whole different story."

Walid's face drops and he backs up into the cigarette shelf behind him. A pack of Marlboros falls to the floor.

Satan twists off the cap. "Hey, between you and me," he says to Walid who's shaking, "I thought that bitch had it coming."

He brings the bottle to my lips. This must be how he took control of Beth. She was wasted.

I fight Satan, using all I've got to keep my lips sealed. The whiskey spills everywhere, the counter, floor, soaking my shirt. He opens my mouth and I down three gulps before he pulls the bottle away.

"Now, look what I did." Satan chuckles and grabs a lighter from the counter. He flicks the flame on.

"Careful, careful," Walid says.

Satan sets flame to the counter and pushes over a shelf, blocking the employee door. He douses it with the rest of the whiskey and sets it ablaze. "Your kids, however. That's some fucked-up shit." He throws the empty bottle at the dozens stacked near the front, spraying alcohol everywhere.

We leave the store, the bell dinging, the fire warming our retreat.

I'm barely ten feet from the door when an explosion rocks the store, the vibration felt through my feet. "Might want to speed it up, you little arsonist," Satan says. "But doesn't it take you back to being a kid?"

I'd almost forgotten how much I used to love setting fires in the backyard and watching them burn. Was it me that just torched the place or Satan?

"Guessing it was me," Satan says, "although that video footage is going to tell another story."

I'm so fucked. The pool hall fight. Killing Beth. Attempted murder of this guy.

"Murder." Satan says. "Walid ain't making it out of there."

Sirens sound down the block. "Fuck this noise," he says, jogging across the street and heading for the bushes past the sidewalk. "We've got shit to do. Bitches to fuck."

The veil of red keeps flickering but the darkness doesn't let up. I'm at his mercy and every story I've ever heard says he has none.

"Ouch," he says, pushing aside the bushes and walking to the fence separating us from the back of St. Mark's Catholic Church with its red tile roof and bell tower. "It's so sad how everyone makes me out to be such a bad guy."

You're not?

"Oh, no, I definitely am. I just said it's sad," he says, grabbing hold of the fence and preparing to leap over.

The fence is only about four-foot high, but I'm worried about the sharp points spread every foot or so to discourage people from climbing it.

"Such a pussy," he says, throwing me over the fence. My right foot bangs off the top bar and makes me eat shit on the gravel. "Oops."

The combo of Satan in control and whiskey has numbed my senses, reducing the pain to a distant irritation.

"That's the spirit, Zachie," he says, slurring the words. He stands me up, brushes off my hands, and looks to the side of the church. Two small houses are separated by an arched wooden bridge over a small pond, only a few small lights spread among the darkness. "'Bout time to get this party started."

Where are we headed?

"The building on the right is the rectory," he says, walking toward the pond. "The other one is where they keep their nuns. One guess which one we're hitting."

Just stop this. Please.

"Sorry, homie," he says, keeping his voice down because we're getting close to the buildings. "It's time to seduce some Sisters with that big ole juicy hog of yours."

This is so unfair. *What happened to giving me a say? I thought I had free will.*

"Fine," he says, stopping to look for ideas. "Ah ha." He points out the 4-foot-high brightly painted pole beside the start of the bridge.

"Alright, so here's your choice." He walks up to the pole that has the words May Peace Prevail on Earth on the side facing me. "Visit the nuns across the bridge or stick two-inches of this Peace Pole up your ass."

Go to the nuns for a good time.

Turn to page 89.

Insert two inches of the Peace Pole up my butt.

Turn to page 57.

The Peace Pole is so thick my thumb and middle finger barely touch with my hand wrapped around it. *This doesn't really feel like I have a choice.*

"What the fuck do you mean?" he whispers. "I just said you can insert that pole two inches up your ass or you can continue to the nuns. Two choices."

Those are terrible choices. I'm not raping a nun.

"Be that as it may, it's still your choice. And just for the record, you're the nasty bastard throwing around the R-word. I said 'seduce.' And I used the plural. Monogamy is so last century. These ladies might be married to you know who, but everyone deserves a night off."

The top of the metal pole is rounded. That might make things doable. *Just the tip?*

"Two inches."

I don't trust this motherfucker. He gives me control of my hand, allowing me to measure the distance. "This much?"

Satan chuckles. "Now I know why you've got yourself believing you pack eight inches." He gives me a second to let it sink in. "You know what? That's fine. Do that one inch and I'll be done with you."

Satan says?

"Yesssssss." He really drags it out, makes it sound like I busted him. "I swear. Satan says."

The pole is about a foot from the first post of the bridge, but at least it's solidly installed and not going to move out from under me. This isn't going to be easy even getting up on there, but I'm pretty sure I can manage. *Okay, but I need full control of my body.*

Go for it, Zachie boy. Let's see what you can do.

Without Satan guiding my movement, all the alcohol in my bloodstream hits at once, and I wobble. "You sure no one's going to come out," I whisper, looking at the rectory behind me, the nun's building on the other side of the bridge.

I'm afraid I left my Magic 8-Ball in Hell. But one thing I do know, is that if you don't hurry the fuck up, we're headed over that bridge.

Alright, I got this. I kick off my shoes, slip off my socks and jeans. I check the pole again, my stomach aching just looking at that thick tip, my finger rubbing over it.

I get an idea and reach into the pond, pull up a handful of water, spill it over the top of the pole.

You should've just spit on it. That's way sexier.

"Shut up and let me concentrate," I whisper as I climb onto the wooden bridge, stepping onto the lower cross beam before rising to the second, keeping one hand on the post, the other on the pole.

Jeez. So touchy.

I can't believe I'm about to do this, but I've got no other choice. If it means he'll finally let me go, I have to try.

Careful as I can, I balance on the post, my toes curling over the edge to get a better grip. I squat down and reach behind, grab the top of the pole which is about a foot taller than the post.

With my other hand, I pull my underwear around my ankles and grab hold of the top crossbeam. I lean back and lower my ass until it touches the top of the pole. I line everything just right and am ninety percent sure I'll be able to bring myself back off it the second I insert the tip, my hand right there below it to let me know I've gone as far as I need.

Tick tock, take that metal cock.

There's no sense asking Satan to be quiet and my thighs are already shaking like they're going to give out. I take a deep breath to slow everything down, and I lower myself onto the pole, only the very tip slipping inside me.

You didn't think it'd be that easy, did you? Didn't your daddy teach you that anything worth having comes with a price?

I put more weight backward. It feels like I'm taking the biggest, most compact shit I've ever taken, but in reverse.

Keep going.

My asshole tears. Satan keeps my mouth shut so I can't fucking scream.

Warm blood runs over my fist gripping the pole. I drop a tiny bit and make contact with my thumb. I did it. Now I just got to get up.

"Hey, Ma," Satan says, totally back in control. He kicks both feet off the post and into the air. "Look! No hands!"

Oh fuck! I slide down the pole at least two more inches, the pressure inside my stomach making it feel like the pole's gonna burst out my shirt. It's hard to breathe.

Both of my hands are on the pole beneath me as a river of blood flows out my ass, but Satan's the one holding me in place.

"Never half-ass any job. That's what I always say." Satan pulls me another inch down the pole, the pain making me about to pass out.

I fucking hate you!

"You...need...to," Satan says, a grunt between each word as he slowly spins us toward the church, "learn...how...to...take...a...joke."

My legs are flailing and it's just making things worse.

Okay, I'm done playing games. You're in charge, Zachie.

I'm back in control, but I'm being skewered, sinking deeper, my hands slipping on the bloody waterfall flowing down the Peace Pole.

All I can do is scream. Scream so fucking loud not even Satan can stop me.

The correct choice was to seduce a nun.

Turn to page 89.

Beth is out of control. The second I open my mouth to cry for help, she'll slice my throat in half. My best chance is to choke her out. To do that, I've got to knock her knife hand to the other side of my body without the tip tearing me open.

The second Beth eases up with the knife, I'll make my move and commit to it 100%. So she thinks I'm on board, I grab a handful of her ass with my left, keeping my right up by my face, ready to strike. "I'm with you," I say, "but I'm no good dead."

"Oh, I know that." The knife drifts back a bit as she lowers herself on me, so wet and warm. "But sometimes you can be—"

I jam my right hand into her elbow and slam her arm across my body. The knife's blade tears through my shirt collar and scrapes the skin just enough to sting. My left arm wraps across her neck and I secure the chokehold, squeezing tight.

Beth tucks her chin, breathes through her nose, and scratches the shit out of my stomach with her free hand. Her range of movement with the knife is seriously limited but she still tags me in the ribs three times.

"Drop the knife!" I yell at her, squeezing so tight I'm afraid her jaw's gonna snap.

She's trying to bite me so I scoot my hips to the side and abandon the choke. By reaching over and grabbing her wrist, I'm able to aim the blade away from me.

Without my right arm clinching the choke, Beth slips out of my grip. With the bit of space, she headbutts my mouth and knees me in my nuts.

Everything hurts so bad I lose control of her hand. Knowing I'm about to get stuck, I blast my hips into her, taking us to the side, initiating the sweep.

We're falling toward the ground, our positions reversed, but Beth presses the blade against my stomach. I get hold of her wrist and force it to break, the snap so loud.

We land and Beth grunts, lets out a long, "Ooooppphhh."

I scramble back, unsure where the knife is.

Beth is on her back, her left hand hanging at the wrong angle, her right hand holding the hilt of the knife buried in her stomach.

"Oh shit, Beth." I hurry over and kneel at her side.

She rips the knife out and swings, the blade whizzing by my face. "Come on," she says, still lying on her back. "Come get some."

Staying back, I plead, "Let me help you."

"You ain't no doctor, bitch," she says with a chuckle. "Maybe you can say a prayer for me."

"I'm not going to let you die." I reach for my phone to call 911, but my wallet's the only thing in my pockets.

"Not sure you have a choice." Beth holds the blade above her face and blood drips into her mouth.

"What the hell," the homeless guy says, scaring the shit out of me because I forgot we had an audience.

"Go get help," I tell him. "Now!"

The man scrambles out of his cardboard box and hurries out of the alley. When I turn back to Beth, she has the knife positioned directly above the blood-spurting stomach wound.

"In and Out! In and Out! That's what my fucking knife's all about," she says, butchering the commercial jingle while pushing and pulling the knife out of the wound.

"Beth! Stop it!"

"Look, look," she says, taking her time withdrawing the knife, sliding it back in. "If I do it slow, you gotta admit it's kinda hot."

"Help!" I look at the buildings surrounding us, the windows closed, only a few lights on. "Someone!"

"Zach. Look at me," she says, suddenly sounding like herself, but a weak and dying version. "Look what you did."

The knife rests in the puddle of blood on her belly. Two of her fingers dig into her wound. "Hold on," she says with a grunt. "Little bastard doesn't want to come out."

I snatch the bloody knife and toss it down the alley. "Stop, Beth. We can save you."

Her eyes close but she tugs and pulls out a foot of bright pink intestines. "Doubt it."

She keeps pulling out more until I grab her wrist and pin it to the ground. "You've got to stop this. You can't die."

Beth's arm gives up the struggle to be free. "You ready?" she asks, so low I can barely hear.

I can't stop sobbing. "Ready for what?"

Her hand goes limp and I fall back on my ass, super dizzy.

I shake my head trying to clear the sensation, the wave of nausea washing over me. "Oh shit. What the hell's going on?" I ask her.

Beth is dead. No chance she'll answer.

A veil of red flickers over my vision, all that blood shining bright for a second. It goes dim, bright, dim. All red.

A dark and dirty little chuckle fills my head. *Alright, Zachie boy. Better buckle up,* he tells me, the thought as clear and loud as any I've ever had.

Wipe those tears, you little bitch. What would Daddy say if he saw you down on your knees boo-hooing a ho when you should be saving your ass?

"Shut up!"

The red veil darkens as my tears run dry. *Remember this moment, Zachie. Remember when you were a badass. When you thought you were in control.*

I check both ways. The alley's dark, but I can see it's deserted. "Where are you?"

Oh, you stupid motherfucker. Where do you think I am?

On its own, my hand pats my head before I can say the word. *And?*

"Get out of my head!"

My right hand drops to my chest, turns into a fist. It thumps my chest hard enough to hurt. Again. Again.

"My heart!" I shout using my left hand to block the next blow.

And? he asks, giving me zero time to answer, my fist switching directions and smashing my nuts.

I fall to my side, clutching my crotch.

Okay, that's enough of this. Get up!

I push off the concrete, feeling the pain, but not letting it stop me from standing.

Good boy. He pats my head and says it two more times, even gives me a little scratch behind the ear. *Now how about we hide the evidence and get the fuck out of here before the cops arrive.*

"I fucking hate you!"

Just a matter of time before the cops show. Especially with you screaming like a crazy mofo. Better reel it back a bit.

"I'm not hiding her body."

Fine, I don't give a shit. Get arrested for murder tonight instead of tomorrow or whenever they discover her.

"I didn't mean to hurt her. You made her attack me."

I'm just saying. Not sure how it'll play out in court, but I'm guessing the old 'the Devil made me do it' defense isn't going to fly. But go for it, take your chance.

This is so fucked.

Correctemundo.

"Stop it! Leave me!"

Focus on the problem, Zachie. Cops will be arriving very soon.

Beth is dead, her body growing cold on the concrete. I failed her. Killed her. Jesus Christ.

No! he screams.

Before I even know I'm doing it, I'm leaping into the air, kicking my feet back, starfishing my limbs.

For a split second, I think maybe the voice can make me float in the air, but I come crashing down. My face flies toward the concrete and I can't move a muscle or brace for impact. My nose crunches hard, my forehead banging off the ground.

"Oh fuck. What the hell?"

Do not use that name. Do it again and see what happens.

I almost ask what he's talking about then remember what I said. "Who are you? Are you a demon?"

Not just any demon, Zachie. I am the demon. The father of all them all. I'm the motherfucking GOAT.

"Satan?"

Yep. Don't it make you feel special?

"What do you want with me?"

For you to get the fuck out of this alley and show me a good time.

"And if I don't?"

Then I'll wait for you to get arrested or end your fucking life because I'm really getting bored and you're testing my patience.

"Okay, okay," I say, looking both ways to see if anyone is around. "What do I have to do so you'll leave me?"

Just roll with it, homie. Enjoy the freedom. Do whatever you want. No rules.

"I just want you to leave. Bring Beth back."

Couldn't if I wanted to. I never did learn that resurrection spell. It's been forever out of my reach, just like Beth will be to you.

"What?"

I'm afraid she was one of the good ones. She was never meant for me.

"You're saying I'm going to Hell?"

Sorry, Zachie, but you've been Hellbound for a very long time. Probably started about the time you spanked it in religion class to Sister Saggy Tits.

"No, I didn't!"

He laughs. *Your story. But that's not why you're headed there. I just said it started around that time. Come on, dude. Even I'm not that judgmental.*

"I never did anything to deserve Hell. Name one thing!"

How do I own thee? Let me count the ways.

"There are none."

Satan sticks my thumb up. *Annie's abortion.*

"I didn't decide that. She wanted it."

He puts up my index and middle fingers. *You were a thief and refused to acknowledge you know who.*

"That's ridiculous."

My fourth finger extends. *Worshipped false idols.*

"No I didn't."

Oh yeah? Starts with a P.

"What?"

Porn. Pussy. A plethora of putang. You've always had that on a pedestal.

These are all stupid suggestions of what not to do, not evil things that should send me to Hell.

Well, the last one's connected to it and kinda fucked up. He raises my pinkie. *And another fun combo: Honor thy father and mother along with adultery.*

That one hurts like a punch to the gut, a moment I'd done a good job blocking.

Your own stepmom. That was nuts. Satan laughs. *Don't get me wrong. I was right there cheering you on.*

I'm going to be sick. This is insane.

Anyhow, this night can be a million times cooler. But not if you stand around with your finger up your ass, he says, sticking his hand down my jeans, my middle finger pushing my underwear into my butthole.

I try to squeeze my butt cheeks and pull back my hand, but it's useless. "You say that like you're giving me any control."

What kind of master would I be if I didn't give you some free will and the choice to follow me?

I yank my hand out of my pants and grab tight the waist of my jeans like that might stop him from taking it back. "Beth didn't get a choice."

Oh yes, she did. She refused. That was entirely me running the show.

"Okay, fine. What do I have to do?"

Start by drinking that bitch's blood if you want to evolve and gain power beyond your wildest dreams. You're gonna need it.

"Her blood?"

Did I st-st-st-stutter?

I kneel down in disbelief, can't believe I'm doing this without him forcing me. But what choice do I have? I lean over, put my lips to the pool of blood on the concrete, sip up a mouthful and swallow.

The red veil darkens and Satan laughs his ass off. *I didn't say Satan says.*

I run my tongue around my mouth and spit out what's left. "Are you fucking serious?"

Sorry, couldn't resist. Here's the real choice: Hide this body or get the fuck out of here. Whatcha gonna do?

Listen to him and hide the body.

Turn to page 53.

Just run. Hurry home.

Turn to page 49.

If I refuse to help Beth over the fence, she's going to lose her shit and there's no telling what she'll do. Try jumping over it herself. Run screaming into the street. No, this is something I have to do. Plus, who knows when the cops are going to track us down. They'll be searching for us soon and the front of the church is one more block away from the madness she's created.

"Okay," I tell her, looking at the fence because her face right now creeps me out. "I'll boost you over if you promise we'll go through the front and get the fuck home."

"Sir, yes, sir," she says like a smartass, throwing a salute I refuse to acknowledge.

"These spikes are sharp as shit, so no messing around."

She walks up to the fence and drags her forearm on one of the points. "Oh, you're right."

"Did you just cut yourself?"

"Oh no," she says super sarcastically, showing me the blood dripping down her forearm. "Whatever shall I do?"

I shake my head, so tired of all this. "Come on. Get in front of me and I'll lift you up."

She turns and faces the fence. "My hero."

I put my hands on her waist which is a combination of slick and sticky with the watered down blood and beer. "When I get you up, put your feet on the top pole."

I lift Beth up, and she surprises me by actually listening and jumping down, landing on the other side like the cheerleader she'd been so many years ago. "Nice job," I tell her. "Now, I'm going to need your help."

She faces me and I just wait for a middle finger or for her to tell me to get fucked. "You coming or not?" she asks, approaching the fence and offering her hand.

"Can I trust you?"

"Does the Catholic priest rape kids in the woods?" she says with a wicked grin, something she never would have joked about an hour ago.

I almost say Jesus Christ, but now is not the time to piss her off. "Okay, just don't let go." I grab hold of her forearm instead of her hand and get my left foot up on the bar, then my right, relieved she's doing a great job of keeping me steady.

I jump down beside her and let out my breath. "Thank you," I say, keeping my voice down, realizing there might be a security guard or dog roaming the property.

"You owe me." Beth moves for the ring, but instead of picking it up, she kicks it into the dirt. "Later, loser," she says, running for the church.

I hurry to the ring, snatch it up, and shove it in my pocket. I sprint after Beth, wondering how torn up her feet are going to be from the gravel.

She's trying to open the church's side door when I catch up to her. "Bullshit," she says, rattling the handle.

"You promised," I hiss at her.

"And your dumbass fell for it." She runs to the window to our right that's cracked open and slides it up. "Don't feel bad. These fucks are just as stupid."

"You better not. That's breaking and entering."

Beth dives through the window into the darkness. "I didn't break shit." There's that evil little giggle. "Yet."

"Goddamn it." I check over my shoulder, searching for cameras or guards. Not about to abandon her now, I take hold of the window frame and heave myself into the room.

It takes a second for my eyes to adjust to the dark. I'm in a small room with three benches, a glass window looking out at the altar. It reminds me of the place prisoners await their turn in front of the judge, but I'm guessing it's for the moms with cranky babies.

I'm braced for Beth to jump out and try to scare the shit out of me, but she isn't in here. I go through the open door and spot her standing halfway down the middle aisle, bathed in a crimson from the moonlight pouring through the stained-glass window depicting an angel with a sword in one hand, a scale in the other.

Beth waves to me and runs for the front of the church, knocking out one, two, three cartwheels on her tiled runway. Instead of turning at the aisle and coming my way, she sprints up the stairs, hoists herself with her arms, and leaps onto the altar. She lands in the splits and spins to me, her skirt raising so I see her underwear's been lost with her shoes and purse. "Come on, Stud," she says, beckoning me over with her finger. "Let's practice our vows."

"I'm not exactly in the mood. Let's get the hell out of here before we get arrested and lose our jobs."

Beth rolls backward off the altar, somehow sticking the landing. On the small table beside the large wooden throne underneath the giant crucifix hanging on the wall are two glass bottles filled with liquid. She picks up one and smashes the bottom of it on the altar, keeping the longest shard in her hand.

"Stop it, Beth," I say, running up the steps. "What are you doing?"

She rips off her blouse and tosses it on the altar.

I run around the altar to the right, but she circles the other way just as fast. I try mixing it up, but she jukes back and forth, no chance I can grab her. I'm breathing heavy and about to puke, the alcohol threatening to come up. I don't feel any better when I look up and see her drag the glass down her torso.

"Woah, woah, woah," I say, putting up my hands. You're scarring yourself for life."

"That's kind of the point." The cut runs from just under her right tit to her belly button, and is deep, the blood flowing. She shows me the tip of broken glass. "Point. Get it?"

"I'm begging you. Please stop."

She drags the glass down her other side so now it's a V. "Beth isn't here right now," she says in a much darker voice. "Please leave a message at the beep."

"I'm sorry. I'm calling the cops."

She rips the glass horizontally across her stomach a few inches above the bottom of the V.

I reach for my phone but remember I lost it in the fight. I run for the door, but freeze and turn to face her when she shouts my name.

The fourth line is drawn. No question that it's a pentagram. "One more cut and this cunt is mine for all eternity," she says, her voice so deep and dark I can't believe it came from her.

"Are you shitting me? You're a demon?"

She shakes her head, holding the glass to the top right point. "I'm *the* demon. The Evil One. The Father of Lies. The Ancient Serpent."

"Satan?"

"Ding, ding, ding. Give this stupid fuck a prize."

I never thought possession was possible, but that would explain all the crazy shit that's happened. "What do you want? What are you waiting for?"

"For you to save the damsel in distress," she says, her skirt drenched in blood.

"How?"

She points at the massive crucifix on the wall behind her. "Bring down this bad boy and I'll return to Hell."

The thing is huge, at least twenty feet from top to bottom. "I don't have any tools."

"Get up there and pull it down. The top nail is loose."

"How could you know that?"

"How do I know you fucked Sally Stanton when she was underage?"

Holy shit. I almost argue about it only being a two-month difference, but it doesn't matter. It's him. Satan is real.

Beth drags the glass halfway down, only two inches left to finish the pentagram. "Well?"

"Okay, okay," I say, running over to the crucifix. "I'll try."

"There is no try," she says in an awful Yoda impression.

I'm out of choices. Out of time. I walk around the altar, and she circles it so I can't grab hold of her. I stand on top of the priest's giant chair and grab hold of the crucifix, tugging on it to see if it will hold my weight.

I grab hold of Jesus's legs and silently pray to him for the first time in my life. *Help me, Jesus. Holy shit, help me.*

"That's my boy," Satan says. "Now pretend like you're sucking his dick."

I look down to see if he's serious. He drags the knife another inch.

I shimmy up to Jesus's waist and tell him I'm sorry as I open my mouth and bob my head up and down an inch from his crotch.

"Nice job," he says, laughing at his joke. "Now bring him to me."

Whether it's the Lord above or straight fucking fear, I'm blessed with a burst of energy and scramble up the cross. I come face to face with Jesus and his crown of thorns, whispering, "I'm sorry," as I hold on tight and brace my feet against the wall.

"Now, Zach!"

Expecting it not to budge, I put all I have into the press and, holy shit, we're flying. I glance back and understand I didn't think this through at all. There is nowhere for me to go with the heavy cross driving me down, my head about to be crushed like a rotten watermelon against the altar.

Well, that sucked. Maybe it would have been a better idea to have done one of the following:

Stun Beth with a headbutt and restrain her. Turn to page 78.

Knock her forearm across my body and put her to sleep with a head/arm choke. Turn to page 60.

Or give up, go to the Author Note at the end, and find out who Satan's going to fuck with next.

Going home and calling it a night might be the smartest decision, but when am I going to get engaged again? Never. This is it. One and done. My forever wife.

Probably. Until I fuck it up.

I push aside the self-doubt and say, "You know what. Let's celebrate. I promised Billy we'd stop by if you said yes."

"If?" Beth says, sounding surprised.

"It's a big decision," I say, clearing the crumbs off my black polo. "Plus, it's not like I was ever voted most-likely-to-succeed."

Beth's smile disappears. "Don't you ever talk about yourself like that again," she says with an intensity rarely shown.

"I'm just—"

"No, Zach. I'm not marrying you because of your G.P.A. or some stupid shit like that. You're a good man. The best one I've ever met."

I nod and study the tiramisu, afraid my voice will crack if I speak.

"Look at me, will you?"

I do. She asks if I understand, if I know how great I am. I put on my happiest face and say, "I'm really glad you feel that way. It's just...you know...it's hard to believe sometimes."

Beth shows me her ring. "Believe it. I wouldn't have said yes unless I truly meant everything I said. I love you."

"Thank you." I hug Beth tight and kiss her cheek. "For believing in me."

Neither of us say anything for a few seconds. "Now, enough of this sissy bullshit," she says. "Let's tell Billy the good news."

"Hell yeah." I get up, take her hand, and lead us out of the restaurant.

We head left on the sidewalk, The Rusty Knife just ahead on the corner. It's hard to believe I spent nearly two years working in the shithole, somehow staying out of trouble with the bikers that call it their second home. "I'm so glad I'll never have to bounce again."

"I'm not sure how much safer being a probation officer is."

"Yeah, but it's not that. Dealing with drunk morons all the time, the late hours, pressure to drink every shift—"

"The skanky hoes throwing themselves at you," Beth says, mimicking my tone.

"Well, I guess I do miss parts of it." I brace for the elbow blow to my ribs. She doesn't let me down.

A huge Samoan I've never met blocks the bar's front door. He checks Beth's ID and steps to the side to let her through.

I dig mine out of my wallet and hand it to the guy, reading the name off his security shirt. Ignoring his cut lip and bloody knuckles, I say, "What's up, Hans? We got a cool crowd tonight?"

"Always," he says with a smile, handing me back my license.

"God help me!" someone screams back from the way we'd come. That's not someone messing around. That's pure terror.

Two men are walking toward the ride share benches on the corner, but they look confused, staring up.

"Ahhhhhhhhhh!"

Holy shit. The yell's coming from a dude plummeting down the side of the six-story building.

The men leap out of the way at the last second, the splat so loud I'll never unhear it.

"Come on, slow poke," Beth says from behind Hans, no idea what just transpired.

Afraid she'll come out and see what happened, I hurry past the bouncer who looks as stunned as I feel. "This way." I take Beth's hand and guide her to the crowded but unusually quiet bar. Most of the guests are turned to the TV screens.

"There they are," Billy says from behind the bar. He picks up a tequila bottle and three shot glasses.

I pull out a stool for Beth and sit on the one to her right. "What's up, brother?"

"You tell me." He sets the glasses before us. "Am I pouring these or not?"

Beth holds up her hand so he can see the ring. "You better believe it."

"Congrats." He pours the shots and waits for us to clink glasses. "Cheers."

We toast and I pound mine, the fire burning all the way down. "Goddamn."

"Goddamn right," Billy says, pouring another for the two of us since Beth is nursing hers.

"Oh, I'm not so sure I need another one," I tell him.

"Lighten up, buddy. This is an occasion to celebrate. I didn't think anyone would ever marry your ugly Neanderthal ass."

Billy's the handsomest guy I know with his perfectly spiked blond hair and sea-green eyes, but I also know he's just busting my balls. I pick up the shot and cheer him. "Very true," I say, downing the liquor, the burn not as bad.

No one else in the bar seems to be celebrating, just quietly conversing while otherwise glued to the mounted screens or the phones in their hands. The crazy thing is that it's the news playing and not metal music videos. The headline scrolling across the bottom reads "String of Bizarre Deaths and Random Violence."

I nod at the TV. "What's going on?"

"Some crazy shit, I guess. Synagogue uptown got torched and there's been murders and suicides all day along."

The replay of the sidewalk splat almost makes me puke. "How many?"

"Not sure," he says, pouring me another shot. "Come on. Forget about all that shit."

Beth sets down her empty glass with a shake of her head. "Yuck. No more for me."

"Bad memories?" He swishes the bottle around. "Everyone's got tequila trauma, but this is the best way to get over it."

"So when you getting back on the mats?" I ask him. "Coach has been asking about you."

"Hard making it to the eleven a.m. with a hangover. Plus," Billy says, showing off his biceps, "with these bad boys, who needs jiu jitsu?"

Sirens outside cut through the low music and conversations. A couple customers get up and head for the front to check out the flashing blue and red lights reflecting off the windows.

"What now?" Billy says.

I'm not telling him and I'm also not letting Beth get up with the others. "Stay," I tell her as she makes to slide off her stool. "There's nothing good out there."

"It sounds close," she says. "Maybe I can help."

"Even if someone's hurt, you've been drinking," I say.

"Oh my God," a woman gasps behind us.

"Make room, guys," Hans says, leading in the two men I saw nearly get splattered. He shows them an empty booth and tells them to have a seat. "Billy, can you get them some waters?"

The older guy in the purple button-down slides into the booth, shaking his head. His friend with the glasses and gray goatee stands shaking at the edge of the table, the bottom half of his white polo speckled with blood, his shoes stained red.

Everyone in the bar stares, clearly wondering what the hell happened outside. Billy walks over to the men and drops off the two waters, keeping clear of the bloody guy who's mumbling something and refusing to sit with his friend.

I get up from my stool and put myself between the booth and Beth, knowing she's probably seconds away from trying to help.

Smack! The bloody guy just slapped the shit out of himself. "No," he says, doing it again, knocking his glasses crooked.

"Hey, hey, hey," his friend says, sliding out the booth. "Come on. Let's get you cleaned up."

The bloody guy grabs the napkin-wrapped set of utensils off the table before his friend directs him down the hall to the bathroom.

"What the fuck?" Billy says, back behind the bar. "You see that?"

Beth says, "Someone should check on him."

"Not you," I say. "They just saw some crazy shit and will be fine. Give them time."

"How do you know?" Billy asks. "What'd they see?"

A feel shitty for not bringing it up earlier, but I say, "Some dude jumped off a building. Fucker landed right in front of them."

"Oh my God!" Beth says. "Right now?"

"When I was getting ID'd."

"And you didn't say anything? I could have helped."

I stuff down my defensiveness to keep my voice level. "The dude head dived into the sidewalk from several stories. No one was helping him."

Purple shirt walks back to his booth and has a seat. "Can I get a double Jack and Coke?" he asks Billy, who's staring at him along with everyone else in the bar.

"Sure thing," Billy says. "Your buddy okay?"

He nods. "Think so. Just shook up."

Billy pours the drink and takes it over to the man. I can't hear what they're saying, but they have a little back and forth.

I ask Beth about her parents and what they'll say about our engagement, but she keeps peeking at the hallway. I give a little huff and say, "So much for celebrating."

"His friend's still in the bathroom."

"Yeah, probably trying to get all that blood off."

"No." Beth shakes her head. "He was in shock. Someone his age could have a heart attack. You should check on him."

"I'm sure he's fine."

The look she gives me says that she'll check herself if I don't man up.

Go to the bathroom and check on the guy. Turn to page 7.

Make his friend deal with him. Turn to page 96.

I don't want to hurt these women, but I am also not ready to die. I've got to get out of here and don't care who tries to stop me.

That's my boy.

Suzie stands before me, the bible held out in front of her. I leap off the couch, burying my shoulder in her stomach and driving her into Kat beside the opened front door.

The three of us crash to the floor. I try to get up, but Suzie traps me in the tightest guard, her arms and legs wrapped around me, the bible burning into my back.

"Fuck!!!!" I punch and scratch, a caged animal needing to escape. "Let me go."

Kat slides out from underneath us and slams the cane on the top of my head, the wood splintering in half.

Two people rush into the room, but all I get is a glimpse of plaid pajamas and blue sweats, everyone shouting, the bible burning me so fucking bad.

I push my hands into Suzie's throat and pry myself out of her grip, the bible sinking deeper into my boiling flesh. I squirm away from the book, but a burning fire wraps around my throat and tightens.

My fingers catch fire when I touch the rosary constricting my airway. I thrash back and forth, but they're piled on me, pulling so tight on the rosary, pushing the bible on to my back.

My body burns as my vision goes dark.

My lungs scream for air.

Satan says, *Later, pussy.*

The correct choice was to grab the key and escape into the church. Turn to page 85.

This can't be happening. My fiancée is a second away from ending my life for absolutely no reason. Yes, she's drunk as shit, but her eyes don't show it, just a strange flicker of red. Has she been taken over by an alien or something?

"Of course I want to be with you," I say to buy time. If I'm going to get the knife away from her without my neck split in half, I need her distracted.

Beth squeezes my dick even harder, lowering herself back, her wetness rubbing the tip. "That's a good boy," she whispers.

I moan, hoping my face is as convincing as my throbbing cock which doesn't seem to care how batshit crazy she's been. "You and me always," I say, squeezing her ass with both hands.

She smiles and I'm positive that flicker of red behind her blue eyes isn't my imagination or some kind of reflection. "That's my little bitch," she says, lowering herself the entire length, grinding her pelvis against mine at the bottom. "You like—"

Knowing it's going to hurt and there's little chance of either of us getting out of this uninjured, I slam my forehead into hers and buck her off me with all my strength.

Beth lands face first a few feet away from me. Before she can flip over, I scramble on top of her, pinning her knife hand to the ground.

She laughs, pushing her ass back against my still hard cock. "Ohhh. You like it rough."

"I'm sorry." I get my dick safe against her low back and drop my weight on her, wrapping my free arm around her throat.

"No!"

Using my forehead against the back of Beth's head, I apply the chokehold, constricting just hard enough to put her asleep. I wait until the knife drops and hold the choke one more second to be sure.

The homeless guy in the cardboard box to my left has his sweatpants puddled at his ankles, both hands tugging on his dick. Not trying to put on a show for him, I point the knife at his face. "Get the fuck out of here," I say, no intention of hurting him but not needing a witness or someone who can attack me while I deal with Beth.

The guy scrambles from the box and runs down the alley half-naked. Knowing Beth will wake any second, I grab one of the sheets in the guy's home and twist it into the tightest rope. I put Beth's hands behind her back and tie them together. I turn her over and prop her up so I can finish the job, tying the sheet around her two times. No way she's getting free on her own.

I lean Beth against the dumpster and fix my pants, trying to ignore the huge bruise on her forehead. Holy shit. What the fuck have I gotten myself into?

"What's happening?" Beth says, sounding drugged. "Where am I?"

"About a block from the pool hall. You don't remember?"

"Remember what?" she asks with a shake of her head. "We don't even like pool. Wait," she says, looking down at the sheets. "Zach, what are you doing?"

"Are you serious?"

"Zach, get this off of me," she says like she's about to panic and burst into tears.

I step closer, but only because she's tied up. "You went crazy. I had to."

"Let me go," she says. "Everything hurts. I need a hospital."

I keep the knife by my side and kneel a few feet from her. "In a second. I need you to look at me."

She raises her head, and I make out the small flicker of flame in her eyes. Definitely not a reflection.

"Now, Zach. Cut me free."

I keep eye contact and ask, "Or what?"

Her face contorts into a mask of fury. "Or I'll fucking kill you," she says, in the darker voice I'm starting to get used to, the scent of sulfur hitting me.

I stand and say sorry. "This is killing me, Beth, but you need help."

"And you need to let me fucking go," she says, banging the back of her head against the dumpster.

"No, I'm in charge. You shut your mouth."

"Great. Now you sound like Uncle Darren."

I stumble back like she punched me in the gut, holding onto the cardboard box for support. I never told a soul about that motherfucker. He threatened to kill my entire family while we slept if I ever did. "How?" is all I can ask.

"Let me go and I'll explain."

I let go of the box and stand directly in front of her. "I'm not letting you go. Not until I have answers."

She sighs and shakes her head. "You stupid fuck. You don't want these answers."

"And you don't want me to let you go."

"Just be happy to know that Uncle Darren has been unhappily burning in Hell for the past eight years."

"How could you know that?"

"Think of me like Santa Claus" She nods to the sky. "You really think I'd let that fucker up there make all the decisions about who gets sent to me? No, sir. We track everything."

Holy shit, this can't be happening. I need help.

"Now let me go. I answered your question."

I reach for my phone only to discover that it's gone. I hope it didn't get dropped in the bar, a gift for the investigators, but calling the cops is no longer an option. Beth needs help but I don't know what to do.

The emergency room sounds dangerous and the hospital's too far to walk. The police station is only a few blocks away and might be the best place to take her, but if she goes crazy, there's a good chance they'll shoot her. The other option is way crazier. Beth is acting like she's possessed. Maybe someone at the church can help.

"Come on, you stupid meathead," she says, smacking her head on the metal dumpster. "Use those big muscles and get me the fuck out of this."

"Shut your mouth so I can think."

Take her to the church and wake the priests.

Turn to page 29.

Take her to the police station.

Turn to page 82.

"Come on," I say, looping my arm inside Beth's so I can force her to walk forward.

She twists her body and tries to grab my dick, but I'm prepared and bend her wrist into a pain-compliance lock. "Nice try," I say. "Don't make me break it."

"Can't blame a girl for trying," she says, her breath smelling like a dozen rotten eggs.

"How about you drop the act?" I say, bending her wrist a little more.

"Ouch," she says, sounding more like Beth.

"Beth?"

She laughs. "No, you fucking pussy. You like hurting women? Look what you've done to your fiancée."

I'm not interacting anymore and just guide her down the alley. The street's quiet except for a couple cars driving around and the crowd gathered outside of J.C.s. They're probably too far to recognize us so I keep Beth by my side and cross the street. I hurry us to the corner and head south.

"Where you taking me? I hope it's somewhere special so we can remember such a pivotal moment in our lives."

"Keep walking." I pull her closer, trying to shield the sight of her from the passing cars. Making it to the station without someone stopping us or calling the cops before we get there is highly unlikely.

"Why are you doing this?" I ask.

"Walking with a fucking nasty ass sheet full of a homeless dude's cum wrapped around me?"

"You know what I mean."

"I don't know," she says, seeming to seriously consider the question. "Boredom, mainly."

"What?"

"You idiots have no idea what Hell is really like. Yeah, watching people suffer has its perks but it's like eating a stale piece of chocolate cake for every single meal. But getting hold of innocent individuals and wrecking them is something else.

Nothing like a demolition derby of the soul. That shit's my idea of fun."

"But why Beth? She's one of the best people I know on this fucked-up planet."

"Bonus for me. I had no idea beforehand though. Just dumb luck."

We cross the street and head west. I make eye contact with the driver of a small pickup. Fortunately, he seems to mind his own business and keeps driving.

After another block, Beth says, "The church's the other way, you dumb fuck."

"I never said that's where we're headed."

At the next corner, I take us right. The police station is only another block or two. A police car turns onto the street and heads our way. They put on their sirens and flashing lights.

"Uh oh," she says. "Think they're coming for you?"

"If they stop, you keep your mouth shut."

"Or what, tough guy? When will you realize you've never been in control?"

The police car drives onto the wrong side of the road and slams on its brakes a few feet from us. Both doors fly open, and the cops scramble out, guns drawn. "Hands up!" the driver shouts.

I raise my right hand, afraid to let Beth go. "We need help. She's hurting herself and others."

The blinding headlights hide their faces as they keep shouting at me. "Both hands where we can see them!"

"I didn't do anything! She's gone crazy!"

Beth cries. "Thank goodness! He raped me!"

Both cops close the distance, guns aimed at me. "Get them up!"

"She's lying," I say, cranking on her wrist, the fake tears gone.

"Last chance," the cop on the passenger side orders.

With no other option, I release Beth. I try to raise my hand, but Beth won't let go of my grip.

"Gun!" she shouts. "He's got a gun!"

"Gun!" the tall cop repeats, pulling the trigger. *Blam! Blam! Blam!*

Three hard punches slam into my chest, and my eyes close as I fall backward.

The correct choice was to take her to the church and wake the priests. Turn to page 29.

In every battle, there comes a time to know when to bail, and that time is now with reinforcements joining the fray. Intense pain racks my entire body, but they're going to kill me if I don't move.

Threat number one is Suzie standing over me with the bible, a bright white aura pulsing off the book. Charging her will get me nowhere so I grab hold of her wrist, pulling her into the couch and using the momentum to get my naked ass up.

Kat swings the cane at my head, but I get my left arm up in time. The wooden cane snaps in half on my forearm, breaking my radius, but I can't stop because two old guys just stormed in.

The taller one in the plaid pajamas stands stunned, but the gray-haired man in the blue sweats drives me into the wall. Satan lets me feel all the pain.

I roar in the man's face and spin us around. With all my might, I elbow his jaw and drop him. I turn expecting another attack, but plaid PJs and Kat are backed into the corner, pointing out the sirens, shouting that the cops are coming.

Wanting to get away, to purge Satan before he kills me, I snatch the large church key off the wall. I bolt out the door and into the dark night, turning toward the church.

The cold air stings my scalded skin, a cruel contrast to the dull ache in my ballooning ball sack. The cane strike did some serious damage.

"Don't forget about this," Satan says, throwing my forearm at the corner of the building, smacking it exactly on the break.

"Fuck!" I scream, hard to tell if the veil just lessened or if it's too dark out here to notice the difference. But what I can tell is that it's me running toward the church, racing for the back, opposite end of the bell tower.

I told you this was all you. You go, champ!

"Then let me do it!"

Headlights turn into the parking lot, lighting up the rectory and part of the pond, the sirens so loud.

I reach the back door and insert key into the lock, panicking when the door doesn't open.

Try pulling.

I take out the key and yank the door open. The priests and nuns are talking frantically at the cops, pointing right at me. I disappear into the church and lock the door behind.

What's wrong? Don't want an audience?

"I don't want you," I say, removing the glass bowl filled with holy water from the holder by the door.

Hey, hey, hey. You might want to be careful with that.

"Oh, don't like that, do you?" I say, struggling to talk through the pain. I ignore the pounding on the door behind me, the shouts demanding I come out. I walk toward the front of the church with my hand hovering over the holy water.

"You really think I'm scared, motherfucker?" Satan asks, suppressing me. He continues toward the front of the church, the veil flickering dark. "You think I didn't want to come in here? These are my favorite fucking places to desecrate, dummy."

The back door rattles. "He locked it!" a man shouts. "Get the other key! Hurry!"

Satan keeps walking toward the altar and giant crucifix on the wall behind it.

"Is there another way in?" someone else asks. "Send backup, immediately. Crazy man locked in the church."

We stop at the base of the steps leading up to the altar. "This doesn't mean the fun has to end," Satan says, lowering the bowl of holy water to my waist.

Stop it!

"You were the one who grabbed it. I'll show you a disappearing act. You show me how tough you are."

He lowers the bowl, careful not to spill any, and holds it directly under my dick. He brings the bowl up, the entire head sinking in and burning black, a sickening smoke pouring off it.

"Help! Help!" I scream, the veil down, every ounce of pain burning into my brain.

I drop the bowl which shatters on the tile, and barely notice the skin burning off my ankles and the top of my feet.

I fall to my knees and look to the giant crucifix hanging on the wall, the white aura around it. I know what I must do.

You ain't doing shit, Zachie.

"Be gone! Return to Hell!"

Satan retakes control and makes me stand, walks me toward the side door like he's suddenly afraid to be in here. "I'll leave when I'm good and ready and not a second before, you sad little excuse of a man."

I understand how disposable I am, that there's no good end in sight. There's no way to satisfy Satan and his unquenchable thirst. All I can do is make amends and hope it keeps me from Hell.

"You don't listen so well," Satan says, shuffling toward the door, my will slowing him down.

A three-foot-tall statue of Mary on a pedestal is nestled against the wall not far from the side door. There's a glass bowl of holy water in front of it. Satan knows what I want to do, but can't stop me from limping over there and taking off my shirt, tossing it to the carpet. It hurts to use my left hand with the broken forearm, but I stick my hand in the water, splash it across my chest. "Ahhhhh!"

My hand and chest feel like they're on fire, but it gives me the clarity to face the crucifix. I shout to it, "Forgive me, Father, for I have sinned!"

Shut your fucking mouth.

My hand's burnt black where it touched the water, but I dip it back in and splash another line across my torso, the red veil nearly gone. "I killed my fiancée!"

The white light around the crucifix grows brighter, Satan sinking further back into my brain.

The thought sickens me, but I take my other hand, the one without any skin on my palm, and dunk it in the water. I scream so loud, I'm barely aware someone just entered the back of the church.

I splash another line across my chest and keep my mouth shut to ride out the pain. "I turned my back on you for false gods! I had sex with my stepmom!"

And? Gonna have to do better than that, Zachie.

I dip my hand into the burning holy water and draw it from my nipple to belly button, which is way too specific to be random. I glance down and see this fucker just scorched four of the five lines of a pentagram, only the horizontal one needed.

Satan laughs. *Good catch. Almost had you.*

"Freeze!" a cop shouts from the furthest pew at the back of the church. "Don't move! We'll get you help."

I understand I'm far beyond that. All I can do is commit to ridding myself of Satan. I need to kill myself where no one will be close enough for this asshole to enter them.

You ain't doing—"

I dunk both hands into the water and toss it on my head like I'm taking a shower. The water eats through my scalp and carves rivers down my forehead and the back of my neck. I look to Mary for an answer, and she gives me two. Her right arm points to the stairwell leading to the bell tower. Her other hand to the side door.

The pond is the closest way to die outside that door. I don't know how I can kill myself with the bell, but it's only given me hope. If I can't cut the rope and crush myself, I can probably bang my head to death on it.

Two choices. And they're both awful. But it will put a stop to this.

For me. For Satan. Everyone.

Go up to the bell tower and find a way to finish this.

Turn to page 102.

Grab the statue of Mary and drown myself in the pond.

Turn to page 10.

Even if I trusted this fucking asshole, I'm not sticking a pole up mine. I'm also not about to rape nuns, but I will have to figure something out.

Satan chuckles. *Is that so? You do realize I hear all your stupid thoughts?*

"Fine. Nuns."

"Awesome," he whispers, taking control and walking us across the wooden bridge.

The front door and porch face me, but that half of the building is all dark. When we get off the bridge, Satan angles us to the side. There's a flickering light in the furthest window toward the back.

"Oooh," he whispers. "I wonder what they're watching. Wanna bet it's lesbo porn?"

Deal. And if I win, you leave me.

"Yeah right." He takes me to the darkened window of the room beside the one lit up.

How do you plan on getting in without alerting them?

"I've found that people who place their full trust in a higher power often believe someone will be watching over them." He makes an act of showing me that the window's unlocked and pushes it up. "Easy-peasy."

The room is tiny and dark, no room for anything other than a bed, dresser, and nightstand with alarm clock. "Play along," Satan whispers, "and enjoy this. Or fight me and see what happens."

I can't control anything so I don't bother responding.

Satan hoists me onto the edge of the window frame and leans over until my hands are touching the floorboards. Being careful not to make any noise, he creeps forward and pulls in one leg after another. He stands with a big, proud smile.

We slip off my shoes and creep to the doorway, check both ways. Satan knows a lot of shit, but he's not that kind of all-knowing. He's guessing all three nuns are together in the back room, but it's just as likely that one's in the bathroom or already in bed.

My feet slide across the floor, not making a sound. I stop at the entrance to the room, the smell of popcorn and hot chocolate reminding me of much, much better times. The couch faces away from us and toward the TV where a re-run of *Murder She Wrote* is playing. Two women sit on the couch. A frail white-haired one in black pajamas lies in the recliner. All three are completely oblivious to the Devil in their midst.

Tell you what, Zachie. Since you won the bet, how about I let you pick. Big bitch on the left is Suzanna. The chick in the kitty pajamas beside her is Katherine. Also got Sister Teresa already lying down for you, but be careful not to break those brittle hips.

A steel crucifix hangs on the wall just a few feet from me. Using every ounce of willpower I possess, I grab hold of it. I shriek as the metal sizzles into my palm, a rancid black smoke pouring up.

The women scream, even louder than me. Suzanna and Katherine jump to their feet. The old one stays down, clutching her chest.

"Run!" I scream. "Satan's controlling me!"

Satan drops the cross, my skin sloughing off with it. "You fucking idiot!"

Katherine, the shorter of the women, picks up a cell phone from the coffee table and punches in buttons, holds it to her ear. Suzanna, with the dark curly hair, pulls the rosary off her neck and holds it toward me, a white light surrounding it. "Be gone!"

"Sorry, ladies." Satan pulls the loose skin hanging off my hand and flings it to the ground like a booger. "I'm here to party."

"We're being attacked," Kat says into the phone. "Hurry! Send help."

"Out!" Suzanna shouts, her rosary-encased fist growing brighter. "Leave us!"

"Nah, I think I'll stay," Satan says, seeing they're trapped, the only exit behind us.

Kat drops her phone on the coffee table and grabs the cane resting against the recliner. The old nun locked in her death throes won't be needing it.

Satan jerks down my jeans and underwear. I'm horrified by my raging hard on. "Who's first?"

"I'll go," Suzanna says. She reaches down to the coffee table and comes up with a steaming coffee mug, tosses it right at me. The hot chocolate splashes my dick, scalds my skin from the stomach down.

The intense pain lightens the flickering veil. I fall to my knees, crawl into the hallway, experiencing the pain as a price of control. I fight the nausea, the pain that makes me want to give up every time my hand leaves a layer of ooze on the floorboards.

"Where the fuck you think you're going?" Satan says, stopping me halfway to the front room. He buries the pain, shoves my consciousness to the back of my mind, and staggers to my feet. "Unh-uh. We ain't lost yet."

We spin around because someone's running up on us. Neither of us were expecting Kat to go on the attack, but here she is, the cane's thick rubber stopper headed right for my throat.

It slams into my Adam's apple, and I'm scared I won't be able to keep breathing. Both hands go to my throat to block another attack, but I messed up. The meanest, most hate-filled face I've ever seen changes targets and thrusts her cane directly at my scalded balls. There's no time to stop the blow. No way to soften it.

My right testicle takes the direct hit, but both are smashed. The scalded skin getting scraped off on the stopper doesn't make things better.

"My bad," Satan tells me, having a hard time talking thanks to the cane strike. "I totally underestimated them."

Suzanna slips past Kat and rushes me. She upgraded her rosary to a big ass white-shining bible, holding it in front of her like a baseball bat.

"Woah, woah, woah!" Satan holds up my roasted palm. "Chill, Suzie!"

Her fury falters and she stops a few feet away, all that hellfire simmered for a second. She feints with the bible. "I do not fear you!"

Part of me wishes she'd just hit me with the book, keep pressing it to my head until this motherfucker leaves me.

But the other little bitch part of you would suck my dick if it meant I'll do whatever it takes to get you out of this alive. Because every second here is one less than in Hell where they feel like hours.

I don't think I can handle the pain. I don't think any man could. Satan needs to do what he needs to do.

I raise my blood-soaked shirt so Suzie gets a good look at all of me. "Don't bullshit me, girl," Satan says with a Southern accent. "You know I remind you of Michael."

Her plump little mouth drops open with a small gasp.

"And you also know Michael didn't look half this good." I flex my chest and thighs, trying to draw attention away from the scalded mess in-between. Satan takes my melty hand and cups my purple-red ballooning big as a bullfrog ball sack. "Well, maybe not this part," he says, jostling it around because he doesn't give a fuck. I feel the pain, not him.

Suzie comes a little closer, fifty years of repressed anger itching to play batter up with the bible that's only getting brighter, the brilliant white aura promising to hurt.

Someone bangs on the front door. "Sisters!" a man shouts. "Are you okay?"

Suzie shuffles forward for the door, and Satan scoots us back further into the front room. He kicks off my jeans and underwear so we can move.

I don't know what your plan is, but this isn't going to work. She's going to kill us.

Satan gets me to my feet, his hand grazing the key holder on the wall. Three labeled keys: House. Car. Church.

Kat goes to the front door, freeing up Suzie to keep up the attack.

"Look, Suzie," Satan says, holding up his palm, hoping it'll scare her.

She doesn't look at it, already fully-committed to the swing I can't block. The book slams into the side of my head and I go flying like in the movies, my head ringing from the blast. I slam into the loveseat which crashes into the wall.

The front door opens. Suzie readies the bible for the next strike, its aura so much brighter.

I tried, dude. Go ahead. Satan hands me the reins and all the pain that comes with it. *You got us in this mess. You figure it out.*

Grab the key and escape inside the church where Satan will be weaker. Turn to page 85.

Don't risk turning my back on the nuns. Finish the fight before they kill me. Turn to page 77.

Although the knife should make me the one with the power, that's not the case. We both know I'd never use it against her, so I toss it in the trashcan outside the store's door.

"Hold on," I say, trying to ignore the feeling of my balls stuck in my stomach. "Don't go in. One look, and they'll call the cops."

"What's wrong with me?" she says with a sick smile, her clothes soaked in beer and blood, her knees scraped raw, feet filthy.

"Nothing," I say sarcastically as I brush past her, the bell dinging as I enter the store.

The clerk, an older Middle Eastern man with a bushy gray beard, stops what he's doing behind the glass-enclosed counter. "Can I help you?" he asks, sounding very unsure. Ten to one odds the hand he just put under the register is grabbing a gun or ready to trigger an alarm.

"All good," I say, not about to explain why I look nearly as bad as Beth, my knuckles bloody and clothes a mess. Afraid Beth is going to split on me, I rush over to the small section of non-alcoholic bottles. If she drinks any more, she's going to get alcohol poisoning or pass out. I grab the biggest bottle with the 0% Alcohol in fairly small print. Although part of me thinks it might be best to let her drink and finally finish this nightmare.

The honks of passing cars are most likely aimed at Beth, but I do my best to ignore them because they're short bursts and not angry ones that might mean more trouble.

The clerk still has his right hand tucked under the counter and gives a forced smile when I set the bottle in front of him. He rings it up and passes me a black plastic bag to put it in.

I throw him a twenty and let him keep the change so I can head outside where Beth is flashing her tits at the passing cars. I grab her hand and pull her along, taking her east toward our apartment. No way an Uber or taxi would pick us up. Even if one would, we can't risk it. Who knows what she'd do in such a tight space. "Here," I say, handing her the bottle. "Keep it in the bag so we don't get busted."

"Sir, yes, sir," she says, twisting out of my grip and snapping a Nazi salute.

"Holy shit, Beth," I say, walking in front of her because I can't take this shit anymore. She can keep the fucking ring.

I keep walking, hear her crack open the bottle and take a swig. She's already had so much to drink, there's no way she'll be able to taste the difference.

Her feet slap the sidewalk as she runs after me. I catch our reflection in the clothing store window and do a quick double take because Beth's swinging the bottle at my head.

Smash!

My lights go out and I open my eyes a split-second before I smash face down onto the sidewalk. The back of my head throbs, everything soaked with what I hope is just the bottle's contents and not my blood.

I try pushing off the ground, but I'm so weak. My arms won't obey my will.

Beth slams down on top of me, and my right wrist snaps in two, both hands trapped beneath me.

Everything hurts. I scream, "Get off—"

The black plastic bag slides over my face and cinches so tight it digs into my neck. I try to breathe but it only sucks the plastic into my mouth.

"Nice try," she says, the words barely making sense, my lungs on fire. My life over.

The correct choice was to tell her we're going home.
Turn to page 99.

Once Beth gets an idea in her head, she's like a Pitbull with a rope. Especially if she thinks someone might be in trouble. Knowing how disappointed she'll be if I don't check on the guy in the bathroom, and that she'll most likely go herself, I say, "Give me a minute."

I climb off my stool, counting to five and breathing deep because those shots hit me harder than I thought. As soon as I have my legs under me, I walk over to the booth where purple shirt is talking to the two guys at the table behind him.

"So gross," he says, shaking off a shiver. "He just splatted."

"Hey, buddy," I say, tapping purple shirt on his shoulder.

He whips his head toward me, his eyes wide as shot glasses.

"My girlfriend is a nurse and is really worried about your friend. She thinks maybe he's in shock and could have an episode in the bathroom."

"An episode?"

"I don't know." I shrug, noticing Beth watching intently from her stool. "Heart attack or stroke or some shit like that. I'm passing the info on because she wanted me to check on him."

"He hasn't come back?" the guy asks, sliding out from the booth. "I'll go make sure he's okay." Either to me or the guys he'd been talking to, he says, "Although I don't know if either of us will ever be okay." He shakes his head as he walks toward the hallway. "That sound."

I go back to Beth who smiles and says, "Stroke or some shit?"

"It worked."

She kisses me and wraps me in a hug. "Thank you."

"Of course. What do you say we get out of here? This isn't exactly the vibe I was hoping for."

"As soon as that guy comes back."

"Sure thing." Figuring he'll be out any second, I pull out my wallet and ask Billy, "What's the damage?"

He looks at me like I called him a motherfucker. "You serious?"

I stuff a twenty in his tip jar. "Thanks, brother."

"Help!" a man shouts from the hallway.

I push people out of the way and hurry over as purple shirt tumbles out the bathroom. He falls to his knees, a bloody steak knife clattering across the tile, stopping halfway between us.

"Get out! Get out of me!" he yells.

I don't know if I should try recovering the knife or stay back where it's safe. "Hey, buddy, you alright?"

The man gets to his feet and slaps himself so hard it leaves a red print across his cheek. "Leave me!"

Beth runs over, but I push her behind me, and yell for everyone to keep back. "Get the cops!"

The guy looks at me and points. "On your knees," he says in a much deeper and darker voice than he used at the booth. "No one dare stand before me!"

"Calm down, dude." I hold up my hands. "No one's trying to stop you. You're free to go."

"And you're free to suck my motherfucking cock!" he says

Nothing I tell this crazy bastard is going to diffuse the situation, so I take a step back until I'm out of the hallway, the bar to my right.

"I'm sorry," the man cries, sounding like a completely different person, all malevolence gone.

"It's alright," I assure him.

The crazed look returns. "Oh yeah?" The man faces the wall and slams his forehead into the glass-framed photo, knocking it to the ground. He laughs and runs to the next one, shattering it with the first forehead bash, embedding a shard in the middle of his forehead with the second strike.

I glance at the bar, ignoring all the idiots standing around filming us. "Billy, get the goddam cops!"

"They can't protect you, you fucking faggot!" the man says, covering his mouth like he suddenly regretted those words.

Hoping it won't trigger him even more, I say, "Maybe wait in the bathroom with your friend."

The man curls his fingers inside the corners of his mouth. I see what's coming and scream, "Don't do it!"

He does it, pulling so hard the flesh splits into the world's biggest and bloodiest smile. I leap forward and snatch the knife off the floor, spin around and shout for everyone to run.

The people listen, but they pack the front door with their stampede. I hear the crazy guy running this way, and I turn to face him with knife in hand. He veers to the right and runs through the small dining section, shouting something I can't make out with the blood gurgling down his throat. Without slowing a step, he launches himself head-first at the plate-glass window, bursting through it and tumbling onto the sidewalk.

I'm not making it out the front door, so I squeeze out the busted window, careful not to cut myself on the jagged pieces.

The man is on the move, racing across the street, dodging a slow-moving sedan. I guess he's going to run past the next two lanes and jump into the harbor, but he angles off and runs straight for the bus flying right at him.

The bus slams on its brakes but it barely slows before it sends him flying with a sickening thud.

"Zach! Zach!" Beth screams, running barefoot down the sidewalk, two cops a half block behind her.

I wrap her in a hug. "Holy shit. You okay?"

She stares at the man crumpled across the street. "Oh my God," she says, slipping out of the hug and starting for the body.

I grab her wrist. "Hold on. What are you doing?"

She tries to wiggle out of my grasp. "I can help. Let me go."

The cops are seconds away, but the medical personnel from down the street already split. I doubt the crazy bastard's alive, but Beth will be furious if I don't let her try to help.

Let Beth help. Turn to page 23.

Hold her back. The cops can deal with it. Turn to page 38.

I'm not going to risk Beth drinking more and killing herself from alcohol poisoning or doing something even worse than she already has. I look deep in her crazed eyes, unable to understand what the red flicker around them could be. Using my sternest voice, I tell her, "No. You're cut off. We're going home."

She stares at me, blood leaking from her cheek and lips. "The only thing getting cut off if I don't get another drink is your tiny little dick."

I'm the one with the knife and ready for anything she might try. "You know what? Fuck this. Go drink yourself into a coma," I say, walking away from her, hoping she'll sober up and follow.

"Ah, little baby got his feewings hurt," she says with a chuckle.

I keep walking, shaking my head at the doorbell jingle. Part of me feels like I should wait, that I have to watch out for Beth, but who the fuck's looking out for me? Who's protecting me from her? I never thought I'd say this, but this hateful bitch is crazy. Had she just been hiding this until I proposed? I've heard of folk doing a 180 right after marriage, but I've never heard of anything quite like this.

I catch my reflection in the payday loan store's mirrored window. I look like hell, my face bruised and bloody, the kind of appearance I would have watched close when I still bounced for The Knife. I throw the blade away, no need to have one of the passing cars calling the cops on me.

The bell jingles again and Beth shouts, "Run!"

I turn toward Beth who's sprinting after me, a big bottle in her hand.

The clerk runs out screaming at her. "I'm calling the cops, you crazy bitch!"

"Fuck you!" Beth screams, throwing her middle finger in the air as she runs past me.

I chase after her, wishing this would stop. I'm nearly to Beth when she breaks left, running across the street without even looking.

A pick-up slams on its brakes and gets rearended by a small sedan. I run past the accident and chase Beth who disappears around the far corner.

I round the corner but don't see her anywhere. The left side of the street is all small stores at the bottom of the high rises. Large bushes run the entire right side of the street, marking the rear of the church I promised we'd get married in. The red clay roof is visible along with the shining silver bell in the tower, but there's no sign of Beth anywhere.

"Where the fuck—" I say, slowing to a walk.

A little giggle that sounds like a demented toddler comes from my right. I cross the street and pull back a branch. There's Beth sitting with her back to a tree trunk, guzzling the whiskey. I step into the foliage and grab the bottle from her.

She leaps to her feet and roars at me like a fucking lion, a fire flickering behind her eyes that can't just be my imagination. "Give it back!"

Before she can attack me, I throw the bottle as hard as I can at the church's iron fence a few feet behind her. The bottle bursts, glass and whiskey littering the ground.

"Oh, you're such a big man," she says, turning to the fence, the church and two small houses sitting in the darkness beyond.

Afraid she's going to pick up a shard of glass, I wrap her in a bear hug. "You need to calm down."

She throws her head back, cracking my jaw, but I hold on tight.

"Stop it," I growl, squeezing her harder than I've ever held her, pushing my cheek against her head so she can't use it as a weapon.

"Fine. Let me go. I'll chill."

I don't believe her but what choice do I have? "Okay, but if you freak out again, I'm dragging your ass to the nearest hospital or police station. You're out of control."

She grabs hold of the fence and grinds her butt against me. "You had me at ass," she says, slurring the words.

I let her go and take a step back, hands up because who knows what's coming.

Beth turns to me with a sly smile, all anger gone. "One last thing and we go home. I swear on all that's unholy," she says with the church as her background.

I've never been religious, but Beth's family are hardcore Catholics. She'd never say something like this. "What?"

She nods at the church. "I want to see it up close. Help me over the fence."

The iron fence is only four feet high, but the large spikes spread every few inches aren't something we should mess with. "Why now? I'll take you first thing tomorrow. We'll see it in the light."

Beth slips the engagement ring off her finger. Without hesitation she tosses the seven-thousand-dollar ring over the fence where it bounces off the gravel parking lot. "Oops. It might not be there in the morning."

"Are you fucking kidding me?"

"Your choice. I guess marrying me isn't that important after all."

Help her over, get the ring, and hurry out the church's parking lot. Turn to page 67.

Make her stay back while I retrieve the ring and jump right back. Turn to page 18.

I have no idea how heavy that statue is and if I could carry it with my wrecked forearm and blackened hands, the skin all bubbled up and burnt.

"Bell tower," I say out loud just to prove I'm the one making the decision.

Satan doesn't try to stop me, but my injuries are more than enough to slow me.

"Son! Please stop," a priest call from the back of the church, a cop on either side of him. "Let us help you."

"Stay away!" I scream as the last drops of holy water burn rivulets down my neck. "Or you're next."

I head into the stairwell, each step so difficult.

How cute. Zachie, the poor martyr.

I ignore Satan and keep marching.

March? More like ninety-year-old cripple motherfucker crawl.

"Fuck you." I grab hold of the railing, leaving a bloody and black trail behind. "I'm in control."

When the wave of nausea passes and I'm not afraid of collapsing down the stairs, I continue my climb.

Voices talk inside the church, but no one follows me up. "We're on our own," I say, climbing the last steps and entering the bell tower with its four open walls, thick brick posts on each of the four corners. A giant silver bell fills the tower, its beautiful bright white glow assuring me I made the right choice.

There aren't any tools miraculously lying about that would allow me to cut the thick rope and headbanging it to death sounds awful. I suppose I could dive headfirst into the concrete below, but this bell seems best. Maybe there's a way I can use it to go out with a blessing.

I limp halfway around the bell, stopping when I catch sight of the harbor. Oh, how different it looks in the span of a few hours. A lifetime ago.

Oh, boo hoo.

Not because I have a plan, just because I hate this motherfucker so much, I push on the bottom of the bell. My

hands smoke, the bell growing brighter as I press, the broken
bone threatening to tear through my forearm. "Leave me!"

I let the bell go and it swings back at me with a small bong.

There's not much space between me and the wall. If I can
get this swinging far enough, I can bring down the entire
structure. I press my right foot against the bottom lip, my sole
burning as I shove it away a little further, aiming exactly for the
opposite corner.

The bell clangs and flies back at me, no room for kicking.
As it swings away, I give it my all and leap onto the bell
increasing momentum. The metal cooks my chest and arms,
every inch of my body that's pressed against it.

We *bong* just a few inches away from crashing into the far
corner, my entire body vibrating as we swing back.

My flesh is fused to the silver, but I pry my legs loose so I
can push off the post behind me and drop from the bell. It's
flying for the far corner as I scramble to my feet.

The bell stops just shy of hitting the bricks, the *bong* of the
bell so loud.

Nicely done, Satan says as the bell heads right for me.
You're still fucked for eternity.

I line up my head so it'll be smashed between the bell and
wall. "We'll see."

That sucked. Maybe I should have tried:

Grab the statue of Mary and drown myself in the pond.

Turn to page 10.

Or I could return to the main branch and attempt to:

Have sex in order to get the knife from Beth.

Turn to page 16.

Stun her with a headbutt and restrain her.

Turn to page 78

Or give up and go to the Author Note at the end and find out who Satan's going to fuck with next.

Author Note

This book was almost the first in a new *Doomed to Die* series, but with thirty-plus *Try Not to Die* titles still in the works, I figured I should probably finish one nightmare before starting another.

At first, I planned to co-write it, but during a summer trip through Europe the story just... took over. The writing poured out, fast and fierce, as if I'd tapped straight into my inner Satan. I'd been nervous about tackling my first solo *Try Not to Die*, but that vanished the moment I remembered I had Andrew Najberg on my side. His edits, insights, and unflinching honesty helped shape this into something I'm proud to unleash.

Andrew already crushed it with *TNTD: In the Shadowlands* with its eight endings, and he's following it up with another *Try Not to Die* and a story for the *Who's Satan Inside?* anthology (read on the next page). Having editors like Andrew, Renee DeCamillis, and P.W. Feutz, people who know this world inside and out, makes every book stronger and keeps me from losing my mind.

A huge thank you to Micha, my friend and the book's dedicatee. While vacationing together, he listened to my unfiltered ramblings, kept me grounded, and tossed in two killer death ideas—the bottle in the bar and the falling cross. Those scenes hit harder because of him. And on top of that, he's just a solid human who checks in even when life gets difficult.

And finally, thanks to my parents for giving me the religious foundation I've been gleefully corrupting ever since. Sundays at church, Mondays at CCD, four years of Catholic high school. Without all that, there wouldn't be *Ain't No Messiah*, *25 Perfect Days*, *Our Fucked-Up Little Family* (coming 2026), or this delightful descent into darkness.

Mark

WANT TO SEE HOW FAR THE DARKNESS GOES?

With Satan Inside is only the beginning.

Who's Satan Inside? is an upcoming extreme horror anthology expanding this world even further—ten twisted new stories exploring temptation, corruption, possession, and evil's many faces.

Written by ten authors from the *Try Not to Die* universe, each story descends deeper into what happens when the danger isn't outside…

…it's already within.

👉 **Preorder *Who's Satan Inside?***
🔥 **Coming Early 2026**
Follow Satan's misadventures.

⚠ *For mature audiences only.*

Read the first story on the next page.

Chef's Choice

By Andrew Najberg

When I open the door to the roof, the night air washes the sweat from my forehead and neck like a blessing. It's been a night. Ho, boy, it's been a night; my shift's almost over and I'm just now stepping out for a break. My hands are still shaking.

In the dining space beneath my feet, that guy and his gal are finishing their wine. Damn engagement dinner. It's not their fault; the couple didn't know the head chef called in "sick" despite the fact that we all know his coke addiction is reaching critical mass, and the couple didn't know that Cindy, the sous chef the whole staff calls the Buffalo Bitch behind her back, is an absolute dick who dumped half the restaurant's customers on me so she could focus on 'the big spender.'

Regardless, I'm still pretty green; half the shit I sent out was over or undercooked, and my presentation could have been bested by a toddler. I'm just glad I made it this far without making someone sick. My shift is almost over, and this is the first chance I've had to step away.

Fucking stars. I walk to the roof's edge and look for Orion's belt. You guys don't give a fuck. You just burn, burn, burn, every one of you hot as hell but a universe of cold making you utterly alone.

I pull a pack of smokes from my pocket. I know I should quit, but I'd rather be addicted to these than coke like the damn head chef, so I pluck one out the pack and slap its filter against the cement rail.

I raise my eyes to the North Star. "Trust me, I know the feeling," I say as I put the cigarette between my lips, light it, and drag. The wobbling oval of the Bic flame leaves green smudges in my vision that I try to blink away as I look out over the city street. The folk beneath are all sorts trudging about their way; some in bright clothes, some dark, some holding the hands of children or with their arms around presumed partners. No doubt all sorts of conversations are going about all sorts of concerns, but I can't hear any of them from up here. Six floors is not a lot when compared to something like the Empire State building, but it's like the distance to the stars sometimes when it comes to the human voice.

The shrill screech of my sister's ring tone, her favorite screaming goats, startles the hell out of me and I blurt, "Gah." The cigarette falls from my lips and rolls over the edge of the railing, plummeting to the sidewalk below. I lean over the edge for a second, but I jerk back because if it does hit someone, I don't want them to look up and see me.

Instead, I take a step back and answer my sister.

She sounds tired as she says, "Hey Vince, I'm sure you're wrist deep in sizzling chicken or something, so I'll be quick. Wanted to let you know that I'll be like twenty minutes late picking you up today."

"But the concert—"

"Yeah, I know. You're gonna be late, but I gotta pick up some new meds for Mom, and you're going to deal with it."

"Glad I can count on you, Sis. Not like the tickets didn't cost hundreds of dollars."

She hangs up, and I pocket my phone. She could have run errands earlier. Not that it matters. Could've, but didn't, the latter being the key part.

I turn back to the rail, pulling out another cigarette. I'll be late getting back, but Cindy can fuck herself. This is not my night. All those folk in the street below have no idea.

I smirk as the engagement couple steps out onto the sidewalk. They are glowing like streetlights, and a tiny part of me perks up. At least someone had a fabulous night, and I supposed I helped make it happen.

I'm raising the cigarette to my lips when I hear the strangest sound: a long cry getting rapidly louder. I look up to see what looks like a huge bag of trash or a giant teddy bear or something plummeting from a roof down the street.

Except that it's flailing its arms and legs.

Holy shit.

I close my eyes right before impact.

The scream cuts off in the same instant as the *thump*.

The thump is sickening, a combination of a flour sack being slammed on the counter and someone dropping a huge bowl of Jello. When I open my eyes, the sidewalk eight feet in every direction from the site is an angry Jackson Pollock painting.

The whole world is frozen, a still life of city life. A homeless man with a bushy beard and a hood dipped over his eyes crouches in a doorway with a cardboard sign I can't read from here. Two men stand immobilized, their attention locked on the blood, their mouths agog. Everyone on the sidewalk seems to have stopped midstride, and every car has their brakes lit.

Someone screams, some people run, some back away. A woman in a blue dress throws up without bending over.

My eyes go back to the remains, and my pulse throbs in my temples. I've never seen anything like this. Never wanted to see anything like this. My blood pressure is so high that my vision seems like it's stained red, and my heart is in my throat.

I step away from the edge and tug my collar away from my neck. I can't breathe. Sweat pours from my temples and down the middle of my back, and my lower back is a puddle. My hands shake so bad that when I pull out my pack of cigarettes, one of them shimmies out the open spot. It's almost a small mercy until I discover how hard it is to aim my lips to catch them.

Someone died. Oh my god, someone just died right in front of me.

I finally get my cigarette lit right when someone clears their throat behind me.

"Gah," I blurt, and I spin.

Cindy's standing in the stairwell doorway with her arms crossed. She is a formidable person. Pretty tall. Not big, but clearly strong and knows it. Her curly hair is in a tight ponytail. She's still wearing her apron, the front of it smeared with blood and grease. For a moment, I think that maybe she'd been sprayed by the body.

"What the hell do you think you're doing?" Cindy snaps. "You said you had to hit the head."

I almost think I hear a distant laugh in the back of my mind, and I find myself muttering, "I'll hit you in the head."

Cindy's eyes widen and her cheeks puff for an instant as she lets out a stunned breath.

"What the fuck did you say?"

I know that what I say next matters. I know I can still salvage this. That I can pretend like she misheard me. 'I said I needed to clear my head' will work. Those words are so clear in my mind, as clear as the sound of that body hitting the street. I tell my mouth to form those words. Tell my lungs to blow the air across my vocal cords to form those sounds.

Somewhere between brain and destination, things change.

The redness in my vision darkens like all the blood in my head surged into my eyes, and a fire wells inside me like no anger I've ever experienced. I step forward one and continue one step for each word I speak as I point right at her face: "I said, 'I. Will. Hit. You. In. The. Head. Buffalo. Bitch.'"

The color drains from Cindy's face. Her eyes are wide as the plates we send the food out on. The light reflecting in her eyes seems to tremble, but it's the pupils underneath that shake. Her arms drop, and she reaches back with her left hand to brace herself on the open door frame. I don't know what's come over me. I've lowered my eyes to Cindy the whole time I've worked here.

It's about time you stood up for yourself, the thought rises inside me, but it's almost like someone else's thought. I even hear it in someone else's voice, a sharp, snide voice dripping with disdain.

I've got to get a hold of myself. I don't think I can save my job, but this isn't me. I press my lips together, suck a deep breath through my nose, and exhale slowly through my mouth. The red swimming in my vision fades, and my shoulders drop a little.

Cindy seems to recognize that my immediate threat has deflated, because her stunned composure slides away like melted cheese from an overloaded pizza. Her features harden.

"You fucked up boy," she says.

The red not only returns to my vision, it slams down on me like a gate. The fire that had been inside me moments before swells into a raging inferno. I'm not just dripping sweat. I'm a waterfall. My breath accelerates, and I realize I've got a throbbing erection unlike anything I've ever felt.

"Oh, we've not fucked yet," I hear myself say, my hands clenching into fists.

"W-what the hell is w-wrong with you?" Cindy stammers, taking two steps back for the stairs, her hand now groping behind her for the railing. "I'm g-going to c-call the c-cops!"

"Tell them to bring their batons. I can think of some great places for them to put those," my voice says – but it's not my voice. It's not me. I scream internally for myself to stop, but I don't control my own body. A deranged laughter echoes in my head as my legs close the last distance to Cindy.

My momentum stops inches from her. I can feel a field of fear radiating off her body mixing with a wave of lust radiating from mine. My mouth is inches from her nose, close enough she must feel the heat of my breath. It stinks of sulfur. Somehow, I can see that all the muscles of her face are locked with terror – the tendons tremble. Her whole being tremors.

The roof door swings shut behind me, blown by the wind perhaps, closing us in the stairwell. Its clanging latch echoes, and the tiny space feels still as a tomb. My tongue licks my lips as if the idea is delicious, and against every effort to make myself stop, my hands fumble at my belt buckle.

Cindy says, "What—"

The shrill shriek of a goat splinters this cursed moment. *Aaaaah! Aaaaah! Aaaaah!*

Cindy's body jolts like a rabbit at a sharp noise.

Her foot comes down on the edge of the top step. Her body wobbles for one precious second and every atom of her seems to beam with cold realization. Her arms pinwheel. One of her feet swings up and then the other. For an instant, she is airborne over the stairs, cascading backwards, her head outrunning her ponytail in its descent.

I don't know if it's my own reflex or whatever force has been controlling me, but my hand launches forward to catch the ponytail like it's a safety line or something. My fingers close around the hair just outward from the rubber band. Cindy's body spins as her momentum lurches against the sudden stop.

There is a wet velcro sound, and her scalp separates from her skull, extending away from her like a tent. She cries out, her short shriek joining the still screaming goats. A whole bunch of her hair breaks, enough that the remaining strands slip from my fingers.

She hits the stairs with her chest and her chin simultaneously, her head bent back like a skydiver's. I hear the tear of the skin of her neck. The back of her head presses against her spine between the shoulder blades as blood sprays from the rip. Her body jostles as it slides down step after step to the landing.

When it hits, for a moment her whole being is rigid, pulled backward by seized muscles like an arthritic claw. The puddle of blood around her expands in surges as her heart throws spurts out of her.

Then, her body relaxes. Her mouth, a rictus of agony, eases back into a state of calm I've never seen on her before. Her foot spasms a couple times, and then it's clear that Cindy has left this world.

I stand staring, my chest heaving with labored breath, my buckle still half unclasped. The goats have stopped screaming, and I look stupidly at the corner of the phone sticking out of my pocket. The red in my vision abates a bit, as does the swirling inferno inside of me.

Well, son of a bitch, a voice inside me says, *we were about to have some fun.*

I have absolutely no doubt: that voice is not me.

My eyes are still locked on Cindy's body, and the voice continues, *Well, I guess son of a bitch is wrong. Do people say bitch of a bitch?*

When my voice says, "She's dead. She's fucking dead," it startles me because I'd expected to only think it. I didn't know I had control of my voice again.

Eh, relax, it was an accident. Startled by a fucking goat scream. She wouldn't do real well in my world—

"But I was about to...I was trying to..." but I can't even get myself to say it. That wasn't me. That couldn't be me. No.

Yeah, but we didn't get to okay? Rub it in, ya dick.

"The hell is wrong with me?" I mumble, slumping against the rail.

You got that right. The hell IS wrong with you. Could've worded it better myself, but you apes have always sounded best bellowing incoherently in sulfuric acid.

My heart pounds in my chest. My palms are cold and clammy.

"Who are you?" I ask.

I am your father.

I frown. My father lives outside Muncie, Indiana. He grows corn and soybeans that the government pays him to let rot.

"Dad's still alive. I talked to him yes—"

Unholy shit, you lice-swarmed codpiece, no I'm not your fucking father. What the hell kind of syphilitic discharge have I possessed?

Possessed? Oh hell. Everything falls into place, and I understand why I reacted that way to Cindy.

"You're a demon?"

No, I'm your mom's unwashed boobcheese. Scraped myself from under there reaaaaal good. And OF FUCKING COURSE I'm a demon. I'm THE demon.

I don't have to push it further. There isn't that much gray area in that.

"Why me?" I ask.

Because you're the kind of whiny little dipshit who snivels 'why me' when you should shake your fists at the heavens and shout, "Let's have some fucking fun." Because every fucking once in a while I get to step the fuck out and put on a little rock concert of sex and violence for myself and almost-innocent little queef vapors like yourself make the best stars. I mean come on!

My neck tilts down of its own accord, and my eyes lock on Cindy's face. The blood around her head has expanded to a near circle, and her hair has broken out of its ponytail and spread through it like a sunburst, like a fucked-up version of those stained-glass portraits of the Virgin—

A searing pain rips through my skull, and the voice inside me becomes a hideous growl like a wolf snarling in words.

Don't you think that bitch's name or that of her cunt of a son. Now Cindy...now she's a work of art, the voice says, softening slightly. *And you know what? Your little nickname for her? Buffalo Bitch?*

"I-I-I didn't come up with t-that," I stammer.

Don't you think I fucking know that? But the fun part is that do you know what white folk like you did when they used to hunt buffalo?

"We didn't call her that because—"

In your damn head, remember? She's from the city of Buffalo. Stop fucking with my fun and answer the damn question. What did white folk do to the buffalo they hunted?

"Eat them?"

Wouldn't you fucking think? But no. They cut out their tongues, cut off their hide, and left the rest to rot, and that sounds like a lot of fun to me. You're going to head on down those stairs and take a proper hunting trophy.

"What—?"

I always speak in the language of who I inhabit. You understand me perfectly.

"But I don't—"

Have a knife? There are car keys in your pocket.

I look at Cindy and know I can't do it. I didn't exactly murder her. I wasn't in control. A court might not care, wouldn't believe me, but I do care. I hated working for her, but she didn't deserve to die. For all I know, she visited orphans on the weekends and cooked them gourmet dinners.

She sat in recliner and binge watched Tubi while masturbating to animal scenes.

"I don't believe you."

You think I care if you do? I want to see you cut out a tongue. If you don't cut out Cindy's...

My arms move of their own accord. My right is jerking my keys out from my pocket while the left shoves straight into my mouth and pinches my tongue with the surety of pliers. My right finger finds my front door key and brings the teeth straight to the pulpy, slick flesh.

"THOP! THOP!" I beg.

My eyes are so wide they feel like they're just gonna pop right on out and bounce down the steps, but instead, I bring myself down them, one foot at a time. My heart is up in my throat, and nausea floods me as I imagine what I am about to do. It's just that Cindy's dead. And I'm not. It's going to hurt me so much more than her.

That's a good boy, the thing inside me says.

The burning feeling is back, and redness swarms the edges of my vision. He's right there, I know, right on the edge of controlling me. If I try to back out, he's going to take over and make me pay.

At the landing, I try to figure out how to reach her face without stepping in the blood, but my ankle twists of its own accord and slides out from under me. My knee crushes down into the pool with a splat, and jagged daggers of pain shoot up my leg as something cracks.

Oopsie, it says with a chuckle.

Part of me wants to close my eyes and look away from the blood, but instead, I just tell myself it's really no different than chopping meat. Slicing a little lengua. I manage to fish her tongue out of her mouth so it's sticking out about an inch and a half. I bring my house key to it, but the voice stops me.

No, no, no. You gotta get IN there, otherwise that's a sad fucking trophy.

"That's as far as it'll come out," I say. "It's not very long."

That's what she said. And the solution is the same one I use whenever I fuck someone. Make. The. Hole. Bigger.

I am about to protest, but my hand jerks up and drives the key into the meat of my thigh, plunging it right through my pants, and then twists. I throw my head back to scream, but my voice dies in my throat like someone grabbed me by the neck and crushed my larynx.

Uh, uh, uh – we've made enough noise already.

Tears pour down my cheek, but I suck a deep breath and clench my jaw. What else can I do? She's dead. Forgive me, but she's dead. I set the keys on her chest and reach down with both hands. My knee screams at my shifting weight, but I use that to channel what I hope is my own inner demon. I slide both my hands into her mouth back-to-back so that when I spread them, they'll pull her jaws in opposite directions. Can I even do this? Is it physically possible?

I'm going to shit yourself with boredom if you don't do this right now.

I close my eyes, brace myself, and then jerk my arms apart as hard as I can. I don't know if it's all me or if he gives me a boost, but the motion feels truly powerful. The sound reminds me of ripping the shoulder joint from a raw chicken. It's wet and squelching. Her teeth bite into my fingers, though really, it's kind of the opposite of biting since I'm forcing them into my fingers.

When I'm finished, Cindy looks like that character from *Beetlejuice* that ripped her mouth open to scare the family who moved into her house. Indeed, her tongue hangs through her torn left cheek, almost four inches of it. Before I lose my stomach, I set to work right away. I have to fully kneel in the blood to get a good angle, both my pant legs soaking up the cooling pool. I snatch up my keys and saw the pink pulp. A little blood oozes out, not as much as I'd expected, but I suppose that with her heart stopped, everything has slowed down.

Finally, the tongue comes free, and I lurch backwards.

I regard the red thing for a moment. I feel weirdly victorious. There's no joy in it, but there is a kind of relief. Looking at the tongue and the broken face on the ground beneath it, I tell myself that it's nothing but meat. That once she died, she was nothing but meat.

You know some cultures ate the buffalo's tongue raw on the spot?

Bile rises straight into my mouth so fast, my cheeks puff out. I bend over and spill my digestive juices into the blood puddle. Forensics is gonna love that, I figure, but I also know my evidence is absolutely all over the place here.

"I'm not doing that," I say, even though I know I can't really back that up.

The voice cackles at me. *It's okay, I didn't really want you to. You don't spend as much time holding barbecues alongside the lake of fire as I have without developing a taste for cooked meats.*

"So, what do you want me to do?"

Do I really need to spell it out for you, Chef?

I take a long breath.

"If I do this, will you let me go?"

I ain't never gonna let you go, Chef, but the question is, how much pain am I going to put you through in the time that I own you? See, this thing is way more fun for me if you choose to do whatever or whoever I want to make me happy, but I'll happily take the pilot seat if that's what's needed to make interesting shit happen.

I don't know what else I can do. I'm sure there's some higher power I could call to, but if they were interested in protecting me, they wouldn't have let this happen to me to begin with. I look one more time at the wet, cold thing in my hand, and tell myself that it's just a cut of meat, but the voice tears through me.

No it fucking isn't, it snaps. *It's that bitch's tongue. You are going to season it, you are going to cook it, and we are going to eat it.*

Something in me clicks off like a light in an empty warehouse.

I rise and trudge down the stairs. My knee, my ankle, and the spot in my thigh where I gouged myself with my key all throb, but it's weirdly distant and muted. Five flights, and every step of the way I try to make my heel land on the edge. To fall like Cindy had. Every step, my foot squares the step perfectly. I could be balancing an encyclopedia on my head like those girls on those old movies.

At the bottom of the stairs, I try to freeze my hands on the bottom knob that lets me into the back of the restaurant, but the effort is hollow. After the briefest hesitation, my hand turns by my accord.

I pass the men's room and turn left through the double doors into the kitchen, expecting to step in and find the entire kitchen staff staring at me. I have no idea what my face looks like, but I know I'm covered in blood. My pants are drenched and sticky with it. I don't have to look down to know there's going to be streaks and smears all over my shirt, and my hands and forearms are absolutely slathered in it.

As the doors swing shut behind me and I take in what I assume is going to be my judgment, I am shocked that the kitchen is nearly empty. Richards has his back to me at the sink and is scrubbing away at the dishes, elbows deep in suds. Otherwise, everyone is gone. I look to the porthole style window in the door to the dining room and see blue and red police lights.

They've come for me. They're gonna kick in the kitchen door with their guns drawn and fill my chest with bullets. I'll drown in my own blood as it fills my lungs or maybe they'll blast my heart straight out my back. Who called them? Who saw me sawing out Cindy's tongue?

No one enters though. There's just the soft clink of silverware and plates in the sink. I realize that the cops are probably dealing with the man who fell. No doubt the rest of the kitchen staff is there too, gawking at the blood and bustle. All this started with that man. Was that what this was all about? Had seeing him die somehow traumatized me in a way that made me break from reality?

This would be so much less fun if it weren't real, Chef. Now you get cooking.

I look down to Cindy's tongue in my hand. That tongue that berated me in so many different ways. Made my life hell. The head chef rode us all hard too, but Cindy thought she needed to claw her way to the top by stomping on all our hearts. Ironic that it only led her to the bottom of the stairs.

That falling man though; I can't say I know how all this works, but I'm willing to bet that Satan was riding him like a jockey until he hit that pavement. That must be how he ended up in me. Why me out of everyone out on the street, I don't know, but either that man jumped to put an end to it or his driver threw him off to punish him for fighting back. I just know it – and the voice does not deny it.

I'm not a strong man, but I don't think the jumper was stronger than me. This has to end. With a shake of my head, I let the tongue fall to the floor.

It hits the tile with a little splat.

Oh, you done fucked up, Chef.

I shrug in what might be my last act of my own free will.

I watch from inside myself with horror as my body strides towards the stovetop. My hands reach for the gas knobs, light the blue flames and crank them to the max. A second later, a huge cast iron skillet is in the center of the range. It's black as night, but I know how fast those flames will heat it.

The next moment, I'm climbing up onto the counter, finishing the job of unbuckling my belt. Part of me hopes that Richard will turn around. See what I'm doing and run over to tackle me. Maybe he can tie me up, and I'll live out my days in a straightjacket unable to hurt myself or others, Satan's prison. I'd call out, but I don't control my voice either.

The devil inside me slips off my pants, and with one giant step, I'm straddling the range and the four-inch flickering flames. The air ripples above it, and the intense heat sears the skin up the insides of my legs. I want to scream so bad, but I can only scream inside my heart.

My ass lowers down to the inferno until my testicles settle into the skillet. My legs lock into place as the flames lick them, my skin blackening and blistering instantly. My world is a roaring hurricane of pain, and blinding white and red light shrieks through my vision as my testicles sizzle. One of them pops, a pulpy ooze bursting out like a smashed egg, immediately searing to the cast iron.

His laughter inside me is deafening, but suddenly, it's as if I'm outside the utter agony that has become my physical being. I'm staring out from myself in a strange, floating calm.

There she is in the kitchen doorway staring at me: my sister. Her eyes wide. Her mouth open. Either of those spots will be the perfect entrance for him.

Her phone is up to her ear, but it lowers absently away.

Somehow from here I can see that it was me that she had dialed, and the last things I hear are a screaming goat and Satan exclaiming, *Oh hell yeah, let's go to a concert!*

THE END

We hope you enjoyed this short story from Andrew Najberg.

Andrew is the author of *Try Not to Die: In the Shadowlands* and has another *TNTD* scheduled for release in 2026. To check out those titles and the rest of his amazing work, please visit https://andrewnajberg.com

Now available to order:

"I am Violence" by Wrath James White

"Traveling Wilbury" by Steve Stred is available for pre-order and releases Dec. 30.

Who's Satan Inside? full anthology is also available for pre-order and releases May 12, 2026.

About the Author

Mark Tullius

My writing covers a wide range, with fiction being my favorite to create, twenty or so titles under my belt. There are 21 titles in my interactive *Try Not to Die* series and 30 more in the works. I also have two nonfiction titles, both inspired by a reckless lifestyle, playing Ivy League football, and battering my brain as an unsuccessful MMA fighter and boxer. *Unlocking the Cage* is the largest sociological study of MMA fighters to date and *TBI or CTE* aims to spread awareness and hope to others that suffer with traumatic brain injury symptoms.

I live in sunny California with my wife, two kids, five cats, and one demon. Derek the Demon pops in whenever he's bored and makes special appearances on my social media.

You can also get your first set of free stories by signing up to my newsletter. This letter is only for the brave, or at least those brave enough to deal with bad dad jokes, a crude sense of humor, and loads and loads of unhappy endings. Derek and I would love to have you join us!

Visit Mark's Website at MarkTullius.Com

For More Fun-Filled Deaths

please check out the rest of the *Try Not to Die* series.

Get Your Copies on Amazon Today.

21 Books Out Now

In the Works:

At Desperation House

In Slattery Falls

On Werewolf Island

In a Video Game

In the Tournament of Mortem

In Port Luck

With No Way Out

With many more soon to be announced.

Try Not to Die Merchandise

For the latest *Try Not to Die* hoodies, shirts, puzzles, blankets, and signed copies, visit Mark's store:

Scan to visit the store.

Your Free Books are Waiting

3 Free Books for Newsletter Subscribers

Think You Can Survive? Prove It.

The *Try Not to Die* series is just getting started — and you can be the first to experience each deadly new chapter.

Sign up for Mark Tullius's free newsletter and you'll receive:

- Three FREE ebooks: *TNTD: At Grandma's House, Morsels of Mayhem & Somber Stroll*
- Early access to upcoming Try Not to Die releases
- Exclusive content you won't find anywhere else

Survive the books. Enjoy the perks. Join now — if you dare.

Printed in Dunstable, United Kingdom